Everything In Style Should Not Be Worn

collection 1

Flippy Nerd Books

A Mi Books Imprint
©2007

Everything In Style Should Not Be Worn

ReadMiBooks.com

Comments can be emailed to mianneladu@yahoo.com

Everything In Style Should Not Be Worn

somebody gimme some gas money
i'm strugglin'

somebody gimme some toilet paper
i'm strugglin'

somebody gimme some sorta smile
i'm strugglin'

somebody gimme me a hug
i'm strugglin'

somebody gimme myself
i'm strugglin'

somebody gimme a man,
a woman to touch
i'm strugglin'

somebody gimme me the truth on the business of ants,
my mother, my father, World Creators
i'm strugglin'

somebody gimme the real reason we ain't really here
i'm strugglin'

i can give somebody
my words, my mind, my love, my world, myself

it's all i got to give
and it's all I'm gon' have to give away anytime soon...

somebody take me for free
guilt-free, pain-free, mistake-free, destruction-free

then...

we won't be struggling no more...
we won't be struggling no more, Black...

Everything In Style Should Not Be Worn

everything in style should not be worn

Someone should really tell her to stop. I mean, it's one thing to actually be blind. But to pretend? It's not such a nice thing.

It's a little worse than faking a bad speaking voice or lying about not having naturally good eyebrows or ignoring prophetic dreams.

The first time we saw her do it, her hair had been cut off. No more lengthy afro tresses for shoulder length fro's. It was uneven and choppy and dry. Looked like a brown tar mess. And she had on a sleeveless oversized black leotard top with fruit punch red pajama-like bottoms that made her look like an obese puppet. The ensemble just screamed of cigarette smelling, abandoned and hardened with the eyeballs missing kind of plastic baby doll-keeping Salvation Army thrift stores with cashiers who speak out of voice boxes and yellowy stained fingernails hanging all over old-school registers.

So anyways, they say it all went down when that father of hers married that hip-less smiling lunatic who was surely trying to get in on his will.

Yeah, sure. The new wife was biding her time pretending she hated his drunken binges. But she didn't fool the girl. That wife of his was gonna make the father sign away on something one day. Just waiting for the right mix of Jim Beam and tragedy.

When they went over to visit, her father took them to another land.

Something about Wakesnewby. Or maybe it was Wakesnewly? But she, the girl, was down for it. It was her father, right?

And he invited her sister, too. They were both happy. Happy to be invited to such a place. It was always dark in Wakesnewby with a really nice street light glow. It was the type of lighting she always said she'd seen in her mother's womb. Everyone laughed when she said that—her mother's womb. Yeah, whatever. But deep down inside, everyone knew that was what made her different from the word go.

They all met up in one of her dreams. The lunatic wife, her sister, the father and herself—before she cut off her fro. They talked for a few seconds before--BAM! they were in Wakesnewly. Now some will tell you this place doesn't exist. Don't try to sell her on your theory. She'll look at you and smile as if you have been shafted, as if you are dead. She goes there at least five times a week. For real. But you won't find the place on a map. It's a place of privilege for people with wavy ears like hers and for people that have reaped so-so karma.

So they were in the land. She says it's not too overcrowded there and that the people do not know your name. They don't even try to pretend that they want to learn your name. They just invite you over to have a salad or a chili cheese dog and hot cocoa every night at the café/diner underneath one of the city's best streetlights.

After they'd had their coffee and hot cocoa and medium sized cheesy fries and chili cheese dogs and tomato-covered salads, they left the place all holding hands. They walked in a line. I know, who cares, but that's what she said--I'm just repeating it. Someone's got to know what happened besides me.

Out of nowhere, her mother appeared. But different. She had a press and curl with barely any curl. Her hair was all slick and past shoulder length. She says she's never seen her mother wear it like that before. She says she should have known, from that, that something was gonna go wrong. Looked like a wooden leg gangtress. And she had on a black leather trench coat, black leather pants, a black turtle-neck with gold herringbone necklaces draping her thin neck. Definitely a bad sign—her mother never wore necklaces. After a bad case of diphtheria when she was two, the mother'd officially hated anything touching her neck, pleasure or pain.

There they were walking like so—here let me demonstrate it they way she did. Wait. I don't have time...I have to tell you the story. But the way they walk in Wakesnewby is totally different from the way one should walk here. They skip on like every third step. I've seen her do it before when she thinks no one is looking.

They were all walking down Lion street. It's one of her favorites cause there are tons of apartments with soft and dimly lit windows. She's always trying to guess which ones have curtains up and which ones have people drinking out of iridescent pumpkin glasses behind the curtains.

But better than that. She said the father invited them all over to his place. His apartment. It was filled with hallways. More skinny, narrow hallways than rooms. One wall was neon light blue. And there was no bathroom in sight (she still wonders about that).

Her father wasn't smiling but there was that jovial jokester look on his face—the one he always gets before he breaks into good news. And her different looking mother was very calm on this night--not a bundle of nerves. Even her scratchy voice had disappeared.

The first thing she thought, always thinking the way she does or used to do, was that her father was going to ask her mother to remarry him. Or at least to permanently join him at Wakesnewly.

But that wasn't it. And she didn't want to hear the rest. She won't say how or why but she is now banned from Wakesnewby. There was a royal blue fire. That's all I know. But nothing good there ever gets destroyed so the city is still okay.

A twenty-four year old cynic was what she was the next day. She couldn't stand anything--not even water. It made her want to cry, which she never did.

All I know is that after that she went to the grocery store around the corner to get a pound of chewy noodles sticks she got lost. When she tried to find that other store—the one in the suburbs—it was way too late at night and once she finally made it, a lady with a thick, surly Italian accent and an eagle's beak-like nose wouldn't let her get those noodles. The lady kept making up excuses, she said, and the lady kept scrunching up her eyebrows in the meanest way.

Then, she tried to speak to all the babies from church that she saw on her way home. But they'd grown up a bit in those few nights she'd spent in Wakesnewly. They weren't one or two anymore. They were now all five years old. And when she spoke to them, they were scared. They'd pretend to be reading Doctor Seuss books or writing in unlined notebooks rather than show her how old they were with their fingers. That weirded her out. There were only two types of humans she really worried about: old people and babies. She says the old ones were usually too tired to be mean and that babies are too new to be mean.

Somehow, on her way back home, she cut her hair and then I saw her at the state fair. She was about to get on one of those rides that look like one big circle with too many red-dangling chairs booths for two on them. She was with our friend Nikita.

Nikita said she was also pissed because some dude with a weird looking square bottom she used to work with on some job she'd loved then hated walked up to her and started interrogating her. Nikita says he was all in her business. Must not have had a life-- those types never do. She says he looked like he was wearing a diaper. Go figure. That's just like her to say. But if she said it, he probably did look like a diaper man. She's good at descriptions.

After that: Nikita says she kept her eyes closed.

She tugged on the few long oily black strands left on her head. She pulled them all the way past her chest and when Nikita asked if it was real hair or fake hair, she got extra pissed.

So then, they went to a party. Right off Addison under the hill and near the loud mouth of the city. They stopped by Dwinnie's house and got her to come along. Once they got to the house party, some old lady with a mole caught in the middle of her right eyebrow and a pair of shiny burgundy reading glasses stuck on the tip of her nose tried not to let them in. But they got in. Nikita's snappy like that—even with her elders. And, besides, she *was* invited. Company party.

They mainly went for the food and since she'd gone blind, Dwinnie and Kita had to get everything for her. The punch and everything else. She didn't even keep one eye open like she sometimes did when we hung out after she'd gone 'officially out of sight'.

They walked over to a spot at a high table and this one lady left immediately. Kita says the lady looked like a tall, light skinned mouse—she even twitched and tinkered with her nose a bit. But she was an older Black lady—not a real, in the flesh mouse. Kita also says they started eating her leftovers of shrimp at the bottom of a clear plastic cup and that's when it happened. That's when she knew she was faking. Kita said she was like, "I'm not gonna eat after that lady. She weirded me out. Looks like my great uncle's on again off again wife Ms. Valurn." But then she stuck a shrimp's tale right onto her tongue with the lady's fork and frowned and started spitting in disgust. She said you could taste her mousy soul.

So Kita and Dwinnie got all pissed and asked her to come over to Kita's auntie's house after that God-awful party they'd just gone to.

When they got there, it was crowded as usual. Too many nieces and cousins all congested in the living room around the red square rug in front of the huge TV set. I still don't understand why they don't just buy a new rug. Wal-Mart's always got rug sales. You can even find cheap rugs at Big Lots. But they won't cave in and buy a new one. What a shame. I keep finding small gold earrings and different varieties of plastic rings in the rug. Surely someone miss their earrings and plastic jewels.

But, anyway. Kita and Dwinnie demanded she do sit-ups with an exercise video Kita's aunt always watched. She's competitive so they figured this would be a good way to tell.

Well, she tried to request a belly dance tape instead. Out of the question! They shouted.
Okay, okay.
And she lifted her right eye. I can see fuzzy lines of light, she quietly exclaimed.
Oh, really. They said, pretending not to care.
And she tilted her head back once again and let her right eyelid raise up just a little.
Then she read the words. You know. The ones that tell you not to copy the video cause it's against the law? Those words.

And she kept tugging and tugging on those disastrous red pajama pants that were hole- ridden by now.

2.

choking women

Lately Niema is concerned about prostitution. She's like that. Every week a new concern. Well, now, she wants to become an advocate for them or something.

It all started when she moved to Chicago on a whim. She should have known better. She was way too L.A./Detroit for the Chi-town.

Her hair was usually big or flaired with an extra bit of Rupunzel to it. And she liked heels—all her life. When she was two the parents had taken pictures of her in her mothers heels. They said she screamed when they took them off.

But in Chicago they didn't dress like that. What the fuck was that? The judgments were in. It looks like a hooker, they'd exclaim.

But what it really was was her style. Yes, dammit! She was sexual. A down right nasty freak. But she wasn't really on that tip unless it was her man. Some of it was silliness. She'd always preached about women being too restricted sexually in the United States and almost everywhere else. She liked to push the buttons a little bit, push the limits of womanliness, that's what she said.

One day she dressed up for her man. They'd been having texted message phone sex all day and omg! he couldn't wait. Stripper heels, bigger than the Sears Tower hair—she was little but grand like that. She walked over. Big mistake. Cars honked. Cars stopped. Men fussed. Men cussed—when she did not stop.

The walk was so grueling, she switched to flip-flops. She ran into a friend and they got to talking. She'd forgot she had big hair and a halter-top until he gave her a funny, squiggy-looking expression, a look like he knew what her name would be in Hell language.

She continued her trek. Made it all the way to the boyfriend's. Knocked one time then shrunk back at the voices. She waited in the laundry room. Why didn't he tell her he had company?
She called on his cell.
"My parents are over!" he shouted. "How rude! You walked away without speaking when they opened the door!"
"Well, I thought you wanted me to dress up for you! You didn't tell me they were over!"
"They just popped over."
"I can't come in there lookin' like this!" She pointed at her now unsexy halter-top and the clear-heeled shiny black patent leather vixen shoes.
"Well...don't dress like a slut next time!" And with that, he slammed the door.
Just two days ago he was begging and pleading her to wear something--just once...

So you see. This is how Niema's worry began. The whole walk home they just wouldn't stop honking. Married suburban men; on the corner for fifty-cent, bummy men; the ones from the nine to five—none of them, they just wouldn't stop. So she ran home. She ran so fast the wind tasted like the cement underneath her feet as she bit her nails. Thank God she'd quit wearing acrylics, they'd be a chewy mess right about now. And the shouldering houses with aluminum colored roofs and trains zipping by every three seconds and shabby back porches and the gentrified streets of Damen and the soon to be evacuated projects loaded with dejected wishers and the non-elastic plastic faces all made her knees sag.

That night, Niema decided to look up information. To do a little research on such things. She'd never been nor wanted to be a prostitute but damn. They had it hard. Always being judged by the same ones that would later be their patrons. Always being the outcast of society.

"So did you do a paper on it?" Autto, her best male friend asked the next evening over green tea and Flaming Hot Cheetos.

"Yeah, but I don't care anymore. Jesus talked to the prostitute, 'member?"
"Yeah, if the bible is really true."
"I think pieces of it are. Bits and pieces. And, hell. I ain't no hooker. I just like heels and loads of sex."
"I don't think Jesus would mind that."
"He was cool as hell."
"Yep. True to himself. Maybe he was just a man with a good heart."
"Hmm…that makes sense. But he still got killed."

3.

rats don't go with potatoes

Last night all they said when anyone would ask about her was that she tossed and turned and twitched in her sleep until she woke up four days later.

And even then. *She* didn't really know what had happened but she couldn't stop saying, "Rats don't go with potatoes. How stupid. Thought you were smarter than that!" underneath her breath.

That was after.

She closed her eyes and banged her head against the red and white squares on the cement floor. Most of the house was dirty. How the rest of the family could stand it was a real mystery. She'd gone to the basement for dust and grime relief. She must have laid there for hours before she woke up to see it.

Four tennis racquets, three long squared off sticks of untreated wood and six pipes the length of two-yard sticks. At first the bundle seemed to be unreal, moving along all on its own. But after closer examination she saw that gray rat underneath. He was moving like he was on a time clock and it was almost time to punch out. Its long slithery tail made her feel like a hundred ticks were crawling underneath her skin. She was so tired, she fell back asleep.

The next time she woke up there were five brown mice surrounding her. One of them, the tiniest one, handed her a fork. She was so grossed out but what else could she do. Two were near her head, one by each leg and one near the left side of her neck. What a fucking nightmare! She started stabbing and stabbing until only their smell was left. That garbage burning smell would live in her nostrils a hundred years later. Even if she were two streets over she'd be able to tell you if a dead mouse was only two alleys away.

Anyway, after she'd killed those grimy little annoyances, she got up and went for a walk. Everything was gray. The sun was out but it didn't matter.

This time she didn't float. She didn't go to her makeshift high school and dance with the band's flag girls (which was always fun since she hadn't had a chance in real high school to be a flag girl—grades weren't up to par and some of the steps got a little complicated. Yeah, she was cute enough, very cute enough but she wasn't one to fake when it came to dancing. That's why she didn't even bother to do the Hustle on the dance floor at wedding receptions. Why get all turned around and look stupid doing the wrong hops at the wrong time? But she didn't care. She didn't even try to take Hustle dance lessons).

She didn't even see her One Day Hope We Meet Lover this time. What she did see, what she witnessed was that man. With the empty toothed mouth.

He was White, pink really with mousy brown hair. Everything about him was crumpled. From the lines all over his face to his lips and fingertips. He had a girl. She had long golden hair and the bluest of blue eyes. Her skin was smooth and gave her age away. Twelve or a little less. She was under him rubbing his crotch with a sheer leopard print comb as he stood, legs agape as though he was straddling a horse for the first time.
"Do it again, this time do it right," he twanged out. She'd made up in her mind that he was hillbilly. A redneck.

"Yes master," the blonde haired girl cooed softly, willing to appease. Too willingly. She was the girl elementary teachers loved. Straight A, softball team member. The type that never discussed sex during recess and wore Monday thru Friday underwear on its correct day—gifts of an overly doting grandma who lived too many miles away to nag her for her beauty on a regular basis.

It angered the girl. Everything within her went red and boiled. The girl was a baby.

The man looked worse than fifty-six.

She charged over to where they were positioned under the shed of the vacant park, in the wide-open space as though it were no sin.

She snatched the young girl's hand and began to pull her away.

"NO! Stop! Leave us alone. What are you doing?" the child asked in utter horror.

"Come with me!" she bellowed.

"No! I like it." She positioned the comb back into her hand and began to rub against his penis hardened within tight, faded jeans. The girl was now oblivious to her.

"Git! She's m*iiine*," the toothless man crooned pulling down his zipper.

She ran and ran and ran back home but this time it was not dirty. Was this some new place?

The back porch was closed in and perfect for summer or fall weather. There were so many windows you forgot you were sitting on an enclosed porch. They had half a dozen trees. A pear tree, a plum tree, an orange tree and three others that were there for mere ambiance.

Her father was a regal looking man in his white button down shirt. His hair was freshly cut in the way most Black men were wearing their hair these days and it fit him—not too young looking, not too old. Just handsome. He was six feet three, slim and knew how to how to make his family laugh until their sides fell off. If Mom baked an apple pie and you'd had too many slices and put away too many pieces of her friend chicken for someone your size to handle, Dad would surely make you laugh off your dinner.
And everything was as it normally was. Rounds of laughter, tinkering dishes, brown hands passing the casserole bowl to and

fro. They'd even had dinner on the back porch. The weather was perfect for such things although it was gray. Everything was always gray.

Mom made a joke about the way Dad had gobbled up all the juice and Mali couldn't stop laughing and RaeRae was laughing so hard he swallowed his whole glass of cranberry juice the wrong way.

Everyone was laughing except for her.

One look out of the open screened storm door and she knew. The dead people were coming. Not one by one like usual. That way you could just ignore them and pretend they never happened.

No. This time they were coming in droves. Flooding the back yard. Maybe twenty. And twenty was too many. No one could even handle three of the dead. Not coming to your house.

"Quick! Quick! Draw the curtains. The dead are coming!" she shouted but no one heard. Mom was still doling out jokes on her husband much to his delight. The kids knew seconds later they'd be in the bedroom with the door locked. That was how it was. Normally.

"Mooom! Dad! The dead! They're coming!"
"Oh. Well, draw the curtains, hon," her mother said still gazing at her man with a crooked, naughty smile peek-a-booing on her lips.

"NO! Listen everybody! We've got to completely cover up the curtains. Mali, get those clothes off the line in the basement and bring 'em up. Keep 'em on the hangers. Put them over the curtains. Dad! Dad?" She pushed him a little bit away from the door and closed it. But it was too late.

"Hi. How are you," her father casually asked a man in a black top hat and priest-like cloak. The dead man's face was an off white shade of gray and reminded her of putty.

She wanted so badly to pull her father back, to snatch him. But he was her father and a whole foot taller than she was.

Mali came back with the clothes and had completely covered the curtains in a way that made it hard for anyone outside to get an inside glimpse of the house. But her father was now stepping outside to talk to the dead man who muttered and shook so ridiculously it was easy to be curious.

She wanted to tell him not to go. She wanted to yell and shout. But she wasn't three anymore. She couldn't act like that. Besides. RaeRae had pulled out the Uno cards and was shuffling them.

A dead girl dressed in a lacey crimson blouse that buttoned all the way up her throat, with flailing tresses of dark brown hair, moist gray skin and an angry, triangular tapering top lip floated next to the top of a pear tree and tried to get her attention. Something about her, the way her head nodded towards the left as though there was something spectacular going on a few yards over or farther over in the sky beyond the buttercupped flowers that flaunted themselves in the backyard made her a bit curious but she knew better.

They wouldn't ever see their father again. Unless he came back with the other dead. And even then they wouldn't be able to touch him.

Two days later she found a basket on the back porch doorstep.

There was a large gray hunk of meat on top of uncooked potatoes along with a note smeared in dirt and mud and wiggly, illegible lines.

4.

les petites demons

Normally she used a different small towel for her face—booty always got its own little towel. But today Lena is too upset to care. And it wasn't the alcohol—she'd been able to tolerate ounces and ounces of gin and whiskey since she was ten.

Something about that venture last night, something about it just didn't sit right. The neighbor that had every outfit Bloomingdale's sold in the eighties in a Women's size fourteen. That lady had the audacity to hang them all in her front bay windows like a display unit for all the neighbors on the block to look at and watch—now that was narcissism in its sheerest form.

And everyone watched the clothes waiting to see which ones changed and which ones re-appeared throughout the month. Everyone waited for the formal gowns, the wool suits Jackie Onassis would've liked, off-pink dresses still holding their shape as though something invisible was wearing them right then, smart business pants in a tan color that reminded her of old seventies sit-com re-runs. Everyone watched to see if the sun would ever fade all the clothes in the window closet but it never did. A lesson in patience? Maybe, just maybe that was it.

But Lena'd walked right past the bay window display yesterday not caring about the purple and hot pink Cindy Lauper versus Madonna chenille and glitter halter/mini skirt dress that was so very uncharacteristic of Narcissist Lady's taste and she met Metrois, Victor and Budding next door at one of their friend's house.

"Come in, hang out with us," Metrois said languidly swaying his slightly teen-aged boyish frame between the top step and the white pillar of the banister on the porch. Lena couldn't tell if his t-shirt was white—she couldn't even tell if it was really him or not. Metrois's face was face-less for a few seconds before a vapid blur appeared. Then his real face appeared, the dark brown hair that fell over his thick eyebrows gave him a certain soft appeal. The extra small teeth with big purpled dark gums. Yep. It was Metrois.

She looked around first shaking her head no, then shrugged into a maybe. The street was different. She swore it was two different neighborhoods in one—tree-lined gloominess mixed with something interesting and as dark the brown of Metrois's hair.

She stepped on the porch and saw Victor and Budding waiting inside on the couch for her.

"Hurry up! We're having a party." Victor motioned for her to sit down next to him on a beaten up couch that at one time was probably beige.
"There's no body here but you two, how can this be a party?" Lena asked sitting down. She didn't like the looks of things around here. Only one lamp clad of its lampshade was turned on and the walls were the saddest shade of thick murky gray—a color Lena instantly decided would be labeled Bleak on a shelf in a Sears paint section.

"You're silly!" Budding grabbed her hand and pulled her onto the almost empty living room to dance. Hardwood floors were always her favorite. Victor and Metrois were clapping their hands and dancing but Lena did not hear any music.

No sooner than she could think: *Something isn't right* again, Metrois, Vic, Budding--they all disappeared leaving her standing there alone with two new beings. They were the color of lead--pencil # 2, boy mannequins, both smiling with hair and faces made out of the same type plastic as the rest of their bodies in briefs and nothing else, just gray, plastic, thick curly chest hairs.

"Come on, Lena, dance with us!" The one with the most plastic chest hair stepped towards her.
"No! Get tha fuck away from me!" She was on the verge of tears.

"Oh, come on now! Don't be such a lil' pussy," the other one added.
They looked harmless but their smiles, they were off. No teeth. Just a dismal plastic bar the same color as the rest of their bodies, sort of like the mouth cover things boxers wore.

The mannequin's shadows and eyes flickered against the bleak colored walls. One offered her a small clear glass of something red and tried to touch her hand.

Lena jerked back in disgust. The offer felt like a taunt. "Don't take another step near me or I'll knock you both out."
They chuckled at her anger.
"Who are you two anyway and what happened to my friends?" she asked feeling somehow defeated.
"We are…we want to be your friends…" the taller one reluctantly answered before fixing his lips back into its familiar frozen smile. He dances a little jig around her for a minute or so. He looked like cement if it ever came to life.
"We don't know anyone around here, can you show us around?" the other asked. He wore an expression of worry.

Somewhere in a distance she could hear a conversation. The kitchen light was on.
"Look. Some would call us demons but...well, why do humans like to label so much? No one likes us but--but they don't even know us. Will you help us? Will you show us around?" Shorter one cleared his throat.

Surely someone will help my ass. This shit is ridiculous, she thought as she walked towards the blaring voices. When she turned back towards the living room the mannequins were gone. Not even a trail of smoke.

From the stream of the kitchen light the voices sounded like three talk radio stations tuned in at unison.

She stepped in the kitchen and found a mother, a father and their son sitting around a circular table enjoying fried catfish, greens, buttered rolls and sweet potato hash. They were silent and did not even utter a word upon her presence.
The father's eyes remained on the food in front of him as he pulled out a chair for her. Lena walked over to a cabinet and grabbed a plate before sitting down.
A black and white television was on. Every now and then it was the custom for the mother, the father and the son to glance over at it and take in a portion of the news. They'd shake their heads and go back to chewing. Nothing mattered and this time they had forgotten to pray just like the last time.

Lena wanted to ask how all this could be happening? How could Victor and Metrois and Budding have been partying right in this family's living room while they ate dinner? What about those two…things--those demon boys? Didn't this family know? Was she supposed to be the one to bring it up to them, to help them?

"Who are you people and why aren't you paying attention to anything around here?" She was so angry she felt like she'd just lost another poker game. She'd been on a really bad loosing streak for the last two months but just couldn't seem to stop saying yes to all the poker night invitations. Her totaled loss was now a whopping five hundred dollars and twenty-nine cents. But. There were always innovatively new and tasty martinis at poker night parties so...

"Baby girl, ya mother and I worry about you. Ever since you done turned fourteen you thank you know everything… Just eat ya dinner and stop tryin' ta start that mess tonight, ya hear?"

"Linny, I'm tired of dis girl. Nah I done came from working at dat damn office dealing wit all dem angry po' people dat can't understand why dey keep gittin' cut off dey food stamps and dey be yellin' and screamin' at me like it's ma fault, I ain't got no time ta sit here and listen ta no smart talkin' lil' girl. Tole you we shoulda waited on dat one right dere. Don't nobody need uh baby right afta dey done got married no how... Lucas, when you git fourteen, don't be acting like Ms. Lena over dere, you hear me?" The mother stabbed at the fresh pile of soggy greens sitting near the edge of her plate after giving Lena a hardened glare. Her eyes looked like that of a beetle's.

Lucas dropped his fork.

"Oww, let mama git'it fo you baby, mama lil' sweet baebay. Linny, Lucas show you what da teacher wrote on his division homework I helped him wit?" Her face instantly beamed with pride and her front gap was as wide as her admiration for her son. Lena instantly decided that she had liked the smiles of the demons better.

A huge round light fixture trimmed with brown metal designs that wasn't quite a chandelier but hung off the ceiling dangling its thick, brown chain much too close to the table. Awkward bright yet yellowed white lighting casts from it. There was a sticky fly catcher trap crassly hanging from the ceiling next to the raggedy chandelier light. Even though the kitchen was never going to reach five star ambiance, it was just downright evil to have it hanging there. The fact that the kitchen actually was a eat in kitchen that looked more like a dining room and the fact that they'd turned the dining room into a living room and the fact that they even had a T.V. in the kitchen but not one in the living room—was totally improper. The raggedy front room was supposed to be a living room but was completed with heavy, dusty drapes sewn shut, bleak walls, a pitiful couch that looked as though a parade of cats had come over specifically to pee on it—it all depressed her. She was no longer hungry. She wanted to escape. To go somewhere where people like these did not exist, a place where demons were only myths...

"Look. I'm not your daughter or whoever you all think I am. You all don't even know me. I saw some of my friends hanging out over here and I just stopped by. *Big mistake*, hungh? And by the way, you had some demons in your living room."

25

"Das it! Linny! I can't take dis! Ever since that accident in that damn gym class she been actin' like dis! She need tha Lawd—dat's what she need!"

"Don't you be coming up in this here house talkin' like that! All that muszac you be listening ta, that's what dis problem is!"

"Look, I'm leaving. I thank you all for offering me dinner." Lena got up and walked out of the back kitchen door.

It was odd, though.
The back of the house was just as much the front of the house. There wasn't even a backyard. Just two front porches—one north and one south.

It was nighttime but it was easy to see: this other entrance seemed to hold so many more options.

On the new side of the street Lena stood there was a row of small cute aluminum homes all painted colors like powder blue or slate blue with burgundy or white trim. They all had one window on top, three in the front and were very, very affordable--even right for the lowest of low budgets and they were all the alike—two bedrooms downstairs, eat-in kitchens, dining room, living room, basement hiding the furnace and attic with a third bedroom for the adventurous teen looking for parental space or for the adventurous parents seeking solace from their baby monsters.

Across the street there was a corn-like field so full of stanch fall brown and tan grassiness it called out to her; it made her want to walk towards its nothingness of empty space. Before Lena could even cross the street, a group of people standing on the corner of the neighborhood, aluminum housing side of the street were causing a noticeable commotion.

She walked over.

A sign was posted on a street light for a talent night: come and see our college's plays written by students. Lena took a ten-speed bike handed to her by some guy eager in his black and white bandana and biker gear and ran along to the small college gallery room to see what it was all about. She'd always been nosey.

On the way, she got so lost she even lost her bike. Her feet began to ache and swell like too oblong balloons from the trek. It felt like hours of walking in circles of grass and being passed by female strangers with mushroom haircuts before she actually made it to the school.

Once she got there, her real mother was already seated but not at all pleased. You could tell by the ugly scowl that had become a daily part of her expression. Or maybe she was happy to see Lena? She always looked like an overly exerted owl lately…

Lena acknowledged her mother and made her way toward the center of the crowd.

The white walled room had an earthy, dessert meets corporate America feel but she was not sure how she should feel about that kind of analogy or metaphor or whatever literary people would call the earlier part of this sentence.

The people in this strange room were not friendly. They all wore black leather. They were all angry, too angry for her. She liked to think of herself as happy go lucky but, when there were so many of these types around, one could not keep their happy to themselves—the anger wore off onto unsuspecting visitors like herself.

Maybe I have no home, maybe that is it, she concluded walking away from the pissed-off left-wing crowd and all the poets with seventies-like pimped-out voices and rhymy lines that did nothing to make things understandable. Before the thoughts could lift away from her irregular hairline, Metrois and Victor and Budding appeared.

"We have no home either, come marry us, we all love you already," they said in unison.

"No…you've all tricked me before how do I even know you all are real," she responded sadly. She wiped the stardust from her left eye.

"We could be real, that's just the thing."

"Yeah, right," she stated lamentably.

"Don't be upset," they jutted in, Metrois tried to hold her hand.

"Why are you so angry, darling?" Victor asked.

"We are so young…and if nothing matters, what's the point?"

So she uses the booty towel for her face now.

5.

please don't tell anyone

--My teeth hurt.

--Um…okay. Like *I* care. You're weird, you know that?

--Na. Ungh-uh girl. It's his penis.

--What?

--It's his penis! It's so big—I can't even suck it really good. I have to keep my mouth open so I won't bite him. And he eats me out all the time cause it still won't fit all the way in.

--F*orrr*eal?

--Yes, girl! (leaning in and whispering).

Footnote: Statistics substantially show a whopping 75% of males tested in our studies to have had affairs with a girlfriend's best friend.

6.

you can't keep runnin' from yourself
  --yes i can, yes-i-can!
no, you cannot, darr-linnng!

She does not want a family of her own. All she cares about is her career. It's one of those things, you know. Don't wish for what you want in this life, you'll never get it. Wish the complete contrary of all the things you'd really wish for if wishing really counted. This is the way she lives you see. Ever since her father was taken by the dead.

She is not the type that wants to be a man, she has no desire to dress like a man or to cover up her breasts; she is not the kind who envies men for the power they now so outwardly own—none of that. In fact, she even tweezes the hairs that continually grow on her chin every other day like they are on a schedule or something. Some say the hairs are due to all the hormones loaded in meat sold for human consumption these days. (I, however, say it is from another cause. Some odd six hundred years ago when I was born many people were women and men or men and women, very few were strictly female or male as has presently been the custom for humans in these centuries of late. But on with the story…). She is the type that will not kill any of the bugs she finds around the house. If she can run and find a shoe, she'll place it over the bug and hope it will go away. If it doesn't disappear on its own, she will cry while stomping it to death and she will hold the tissue she's stuffed the bug in far away from her body as she treks to the bathroom to flush it down the toilet. Sometimes she watches the insects body parts flush down the toilet, though. That has a lot to do with regret.

She often thinks she would have done better this lifetime around as an ant. A while ago she wrote in her journal that ants work harder than most people and that they are as small as we must seem to the Almighty. Then she wrote something I almost did not get because her handwriting is sometimes scribbly and too loopy. She wrote that she wonders why the Almighty does not stomp us or flush us away. Then there was a: dot. dot. dot. and she wrote something about Tsumani flushing people away and she started wondering again.

She wonders if Goddess, too, feels guilty about natural disasters such as those. The guilt of killing an ant—such a small thing—consumes her like the tartar and hot sauce concoction she gets up and licks by the spoonfuls in the middle of the night. Hello, even though you live alone that does *not* mean someone does not see you! I wish someone would tell her. It's so disgusting, really. My eyes cannot bare to bare it, no matter how many times I witness her lick the mixture.

And she wears lots of skirts. Short and fitted ones, long, loose and gypsy ones, knee reaching denim ones… Believe you me, she *is* feminine.

It's just that she gets sick when children are nearby—something about their smell and when they cry in malls like un-human banshee's let on the loose, like wild terrors in the middle of a séance, like a savage hunting for human blood smack-dab in the middle of a jungle-like forest of a popular suburb. Kids? Huh!

She doesn't wish to have anything like that come out of *her* body. Who would want to carry all that weight anyway? And who would want to grow un-erasable stretch marks or pay all that money for cosmetic surgery afterwards? And who would want to waste nine months? She can think of several hundred better ways to spend nine months but don't ask her to give you one. She'll start ranting on and on and won't finish until she has gone down the complete list organized in three columns on her list of a hundred reasons not to get pregnant.

One time she threw up after being asked to baby-sit a neighbor's son. True story!

But if you look in the garbage in her bathroom, you can see. (I have always said one can find out an insurmountable amount of knowledge with the quick examination of someone's garbage). In her bathroom garbage (I cannot tell you much about the garbage under the kitchen sink, though. She takes it out on a daily basis and usually she's taken it to the dumpster by the time I wake up to check up on her, early bird that she is) you will often find umbrellas with way too much jump to stay down in windy weather, nice smelling bottles of bubble bath all emptied out, shoes that have lost their souls and white shoestrings, started pottery that was all too lopsided to be placed on the kitchen's recently relined shelves, the brand new dishwasher's handbook, fake eyelashes, some of her real eyelashes, chewed up glitter pens, empty DVD cartons for all the weekends alone, vitamin E capsules all squeezed empty yellow and a wish list of all the things she wishes not to wish for.

But how can one so young with calf muscles strong enough to climb mountains for days at a time be so down in the dumps when there is Vegas, L.A., N.Y. and rainforest in lands that only let you in by boat? Even though she knows there are other places, she prefers her heart to burn and makes sure of it by clasping it so tightly, so tight until it lilts away and spits every feeling from good to bad down the sink each morning and every single night when she brushes her teeth. I swear this young woman is the only person I've ever seen who is completely unphased by anything. Never smiles, never speaks past simple answers to the cashiers at the grocery store. At work she hides behind the desktop and what she really wants to do, own her own pottery shop, she refuses. I pulled up business plans on her computer last week and she closed the window and went back to work. I still don't understand what it is she does in that office all day and neither does she. She just goes and clicks on the HP and stays until five or later, if the supervisors allow her and then, on Friday, she collects a check.

She is as hard to improve as gingivitis.

As her past life predecessor it is my job to protect her. But I can't--how can I work with someone so bottled up?

I should know. I already went thru this six hundred and fifty years ago myself and I am tired. I guess I am getting paid back. After my Anileelay was killed by Horesnisea, I could never again taste anything, the berries on the Pam-Pam tree, the dusty beans in the shells that lived under the sea in my one time best friend Nagoshia's home in the underwatertower lowrise, the Kush's sweet candy tea, not even kind words. Then, the one time I did come out of my reserve and spoke in deep words with Nagoshia, I found out she had been sleeping with Anileelay.

And I moved all the way inside a Renelius-Prong tree in Magolio't…on (which is now located under Atlanta, Georgia but you have to crawl to it, pass the beach and dig until you find the purple people who have hazy eyes that light up and turn into blizzard snowcones and warm fawned honey. Now these are some fun people. They let you lick the honey off their eyes and man does it taste good! There is no other taste to long for once one has experienced the taste of their eyes and for me that was true torture because no matter how I tried to go taste their eyes once more, my soul could not bear it. Not again. Couldn't go there again).

I lived by locking myself in my Renelius-Prong loft deep inside the tree under the 43rd floor, away from all the drama, all the laughs of the purple people and their echoing jazz and drum overt hip-hop bands (nothing is new under over the sun, Hon, not even hip-hop). I missed out on so much lying around in bed sleeping away the Anileelay memories. And Nagoshia and I had been friends since our first teeth cut into our newborn gums. We had even suckled on our mothers in the same Temple Worship restroom.

What genius thought up this game of life anyway? It is a terrible game. Us Indigo's cannot take such disasters. Our skin coverings are not fit for life's rough touches and from life's downturns we burn worse than one slathered in Retin-A out tanning on a South African beach.

Once I finally decided to come out of the tree some 80 years later, everything had changed. The purple people had turned clear and I hadn't heard anything about it because I did well not to keep up with the evening news. I kept running into them, bumping them in such unkindly manners. And I had never had the chance to bear my own little fruits you all now call children. Children. That word makes me laugh every time. Who thought up *that* one? Must have been Sorenika the Female Fenuke. When she's not stealing away the Splegitariecs with her seductively oscillating arms she's always seasoning up literature and alphabets for various languages of the earthly ones in the human tribe.

Anywho, a clear, see-thru person once told me I could get another chance at bearing fruit and another chance at being able to taste without thinking of my dear sweet Anileelay or of that witch Nagoshia.

And this is the snag: this chick who refuses to live beyond routine. She is so angry at her mother for remarrying and not keeping the candle burning on the mantle for her first husband. Especially since he continues stopping by and leaving packages bundled as best a dead one can—the dead have no need to be tidy, let me tell you.

If I could just get her to stop being so tragic and so stuck on her Sade CD's for just one minute! She hates her brother and sister for not sitting and going over the memories before her father's death with her on the weekends. She hates the guys who ask her if she'd like to do lunch at Ruth Chris. She figures they will one day open a door to speak to a stranger and never come back the same and the thought is enough to make her swear off relationships forever.

This is worse than that movie *Ground Hog's Day*. I am her. I am stuck in her space and time and on top of that, to make matters only more appalling, I also am me and I have to watch. Two people stuck in different spaces of time dealing with the same issue is what my life now has become.

Unless I can get her to change her ways.
Then, I will finally be able to move on.

She isn't so bad really—if you take away the suffering.
When she was nine she taught herself to do algebra with college books her mother had around the house and she did well with those other two books she'd found in the attic, *Teach Yourself How To Draw Any Flower* and *Cartoon For Dummies*. The pottery gift she got from me. I have always been a nifty shaper of crystal vases and satchual, psychic enhancing plates fit for a king or lady president to eat off.

Please. If you know of anyway in which I can help her, of anyway I can make her once again live and play Uno and smile at old lady's walking across the street with navy feathered hats toppling their curly heads and any way I can get her to play baseball again the way she once used to, *please* let me know. I desperately want to get this whole thing over with. You don't have to email or write or use a calling card or anything—that'll all take too long. Just say it out loud and blow after your words. That way I can come as quickly as possible and gather up your wordy smoke and change this bind I'm in. I already have a name for the twins, one boy and one girl, I desire to one day create, Dooley and Gina.

7.

how to get your man back if he's dumped you for an ugly chick (Please read in completion before execution)

Okay. So you're staring at your watch dressed in that sexy pink and white little plastic Priscilla number eagerly awaiting the minute your Big Daddy will step in the door and greedily consume his present for being such a good, good boy.

But after hours of checking, re-checking reapplying your makeup and re-styling your hair your cell phone buzzes. He clearly states over the stifled giggles of something that can only be another female, that he is not coming over tonight. Not now. Not ever. *He* had decided it is not working. No woman, beautiful, semi-beautiful, cute or flat-out moche likes to hear these words from her man. Our experts would like to take this time out to express their deepest sympathies. But, they'd also like to inform you that such a statement is strictly due to over consumption of non-light beers or a sudden new and interesting sexual trick.

Before you holler that you have done all that and then some in the bedroom or scream like a baby, throw on your coat girlfriend and grab those keys he, being a man, forgot to request back before "ending it all." You're about to enter **Phase I** of the **Get Any Man You Want or The Dumb Ass That Dumped You**. And, yes, you are pretty but, hell. Look at your predicament. Pamela and Halle and Vanessa Williams are prettier than you and Eric Bennet and Tommy Lee and Kid Rock and Rick Fox still weren't on point…you get the picture. Yes, dear pretty one, you still need our help.

Remaining barely dressed in that Priscilla's flimsy plastic, you are now ready to begin.

1 put the petal to the metal with your Jimmy Choo's and head over to ole boy's house.
2 Turn your lights off as you approach his block.

3 Walking lightly, approach the door and with a quick insertion of the key, you should be inside his home.

4 Smile. This will irrefutably prove to be difficult. Especially once you witness him cuddling with a behemoth of a female companion. She may even have a slight mustache--no amount of shining personality could overlook that. But this is the cornerstone of your plan, so hold tight, dear one. We too have experienced such corrupt injustice.

5 You must execute your most baffling expression, flutter your eyelashes a bit and respond to your intrusion by simply stating that you thought his call was from your sugar daddy. Yes—yes, we know you were faithful and never, no never cheated—except that one time when you went to Canada and met that fine Carson Daly look-a-like and—never mind. You're a woman and being such, it didn't count.
Tip: this does well to incite a morsel of jealousy. See, even though he claims he wants nothing else to do with you, he wants to rest assured that you will pine over him and listen to Keyshia Cole's "Love" or some other awful forlorn woman song. He wants to feel important. He does not want to feel that he was merely part-time booty.

6 Slip open your coat a bit and "unintentionally" give the beast and your boy a flash of the very outfit Champagne is wearing on this month's cover of *Hustler*. Hurry to close it, but make sure to slowly button or zip your coat. We recommend a coat that buttons down as this will take more time and will definitely cause a distraction.

7 Smile at the beastly eyesore, shake her hand and wish them luck. Really, even though she is at best an unsightly sight to behold, she still remains a part of a universal sisterhood. She is not the enemy. She is, rather, what our experts call a wake up call. You will want to be as genuine as possible. You do not want beast face to think you are plotting against her or planning to sugar her tank at a later

date. You simply want your encounter to haunt his and her thoughts for the next week or so.
Tip: This will make her think there is something wrong with him. No woman desires unwanted goods.

8 Place all keys to his place in *her* hand, request yours back and leave once he relinquishes them. Trust us, at this point, he will not want you to give them back. And the fact that you have given *her* the keys will be most upsetting to him being that he was not planning on giving her access to his pad—especially after your intrusion. This will cause great conflict and distrust between the newly dreadful couple, as is the goal.
Tip: This will also make her feel inferior to you. You will now have leverage. Prior to this incident, she was basking in the glory that can only come from being not so attractive and still managing to attain someone else's man.

9 On the ride home, listen to hard rock or techno or reggae—but not that slow ballad stuff. Red Rat or Sean Paul are our recommendations, as you will need to build immunity. Phase 2 calls for a lacerating brutality pretty girls would rather not face.

10 Now within the confines of your manless home, it is time to turn on all lights, take off all clothing and head to either the three-way mirror in your closet or the bathroom should you not have the must-have of a three-way mirror.
***Tip:** If you are really pretty, you should invest in a three-way mirror.

11 Next, remove all makeup and pull back all weave or comb out all back-combing and repeat this mantra: I am *still* too beautiful. Do so as many times as you determine necessary. Our research shows that pretty girls all over the world love this exercise.

12 Okay. Now. Sorry. Brace yourself for this one. You may even want to get a good grip on the counter or something for balance. Now—and we do truly hate to do this to you but it is necessary— you must repeat: Beauty is not all, I will learn to be humble at my

downfall. At least five times. Next, ask yourself one question: Did you swallow? Oh, yes! Oh, yes! We are sorry. But. It all boils down to two things. Did you guzzle or did your spit? Data has shown that most in your predicament completely avoided all oral contact for the mere sake of reputation. Yes mommy told you that good girls did not go down but where is she today? Is she a satisfied self-actualized woman or is she an unfulfilled gossip or nag or divorced or widowed with no prospective suitor? But what about that Monica Lewinsky, huh? She is a paid Bia-Bia with her own purse line. And—forget what you heard—she has a stash of boyfriends young and Alex Trabek old. Public announcement was the best thing to happen to that not-so-cute thing. Yes, in short, you will realize the folly of your ways. One time we overheard a conversation wherein Eric Bennet told Tamia that Halle refused to do such deeds. What a shame. She could have saved herself days of paperwork. But then again, we thought she could have done better. After her next ceremony, we shall send her a copy of this article.

13 **Phase 3:** Go to the mall, makeup-less, dressed down and shop. Flirt. Go for coffee. Pass gas even if someone is nearby. This will help you lower the walls you have built for the sake of reputation. Read a good erotic novella—but make sure it is loaded with satirical humor—you want to uplift your spirits and get prepared for what is to cum. If you are unused to such reads, we recommend books such as *Bling*. After you pick up such a novel from the bookstore, sit in an open area of the mall atrium and read it. Oh—and one more thing. Make sure to purchase *Playboy*--or the like and hold it in front of your book. When a male suitor approaches, you must inform him that you are using the magazine to cover up what you are reading because it is too racy. Add that you are a lady and like to keep certain fetishes confined to the bedroom--you know, the old freak in the sheets, lady in the streets adage. If done correctly you will leave the mall with at least six phone numbers of new candidates. We shall call them Booty Boys until you weed out the Keepers and the Strictly For Booty Calls If They Have Big Guns.

If you have not received a number, try a different location within the mall. There are many areas in the mall that have comfortable seating that are in plain view.

**Tip: You must request a view of the package at a later date. Simply inform your Mall Booty Boys that you will need to see what you will be working with. They will love this as much as you will. It gives you a chance to pick which ones are of interest to you. There is nothing more terrible than liking a guy only to find out you do not like the looks of his friend. A word of caution: do not be afraid of curves, upward turns or excessively large tips. These are very, very good situations for other activities.

14 Watch uncut videos at regular intervals over the next week. In this time, you will learn more about Tip Drills and will become at ease with fellacio, its lingo and the like.

15 Listen to Shawnna's "Getting Some Head." The beat and slurping of the chorus line will further motivate you.

16 **Phase 3:** Ignore his calls. He *will* call. He will be thinking about that sugar daddy comment. Or, if you live in a small town, it is possible that one of his boys could not stop talking about you after giving you his number at the mall.

17 Ten days later or so, when you are ready, return his call. Tell him that you are horney but Monthly Martha has come to visit and, since you don't get down when blood is on the ground, the only thing that would satisfy your sweaty, freaky bodily urges is…well. Here is where you stop. Abruptly. Do not let his pleas compel you to go any further. Tell him you will contact him later. Tell him that you are happy he has a new love. Tell him you've met someone new too. Make sure to include that, after watching *Talk Sex With Sue* and a few upscale Black porns with this dude named Antwan-- or whatever name of your choice—and seeing how big he was, you are now infatuated with putting things in your mouth. Then—you will rush him off the phone by stating that you have a call beeping on the other line. Watch him freak out. He will probably show up

to your home. This is why we admonished you to get your set of keys from him in step 8.

18 Now, if you still want the dumb ass muthafucka who dumped you even though you are truly beautiful, can cook up a mean stir fry, wear a size two and can hang with the most intelligent of the intellects, it is all up to you. This is not India nor Africa nor China nor Mexico nor Minnesota nor Missouri where women have no say on the matter. This is not 200 b.c.; you will not be stoned for refusing to take him up on his offer. Should you still want him, we suggest you sit a glass of Pepsi on your nightstand to help smooth out the after taste of your initial experience. Remember to watch as much porn as possible and to copy such orally intensive moves step by step. Remember teeth control. Janet Jackme is one of the industry's best.

But truthfully, at this point, that one dude from the mall, you know the one with the sexy smile that made you want to lick his lips? He is a much better bet. Not only will he be willing to reciprocate the favor making you a very pretty and happy camper, you two will both be whipped by one another and one day have credit card debt, own a beautiful home within a suburban subdivision that may very well get foreclosed on, have 2.5 bratty ass children that will beg for every toy during Nickelodeon commercials and will go to college on your dollars and flunk out and will one day put you in a nursing home and forget to visit and, thus, live the life that is the American dream.

Good luck Pretty Young Thang. And as always, happy Suckings and good Fuckings!
In our next issue:

How To Remain Happily Married By Avoiding The American Dream

8.

big booty girl

Once upon a time, not all that faraway--if you live in the Midwest and didn't mind a quick drive to Detroit, not long ago (cause this all happened last week), there lived a girl named Aphrodite Marsusala Tamiky Blessed-Be Jones. She was half Greek, a fourth Native American (her mother claims) and three fourths just plain ole African American Negro (but since most African American totally do not relate to Africans from the African continent since that was some odd four hundred years ago when Africans were brought into America, we shall say—also for the sake of time—Black). She was very beautiful. Very, *very*—well, you get the point—attractive. Her perfect, by current societal standards, oval shaped face with the widow's peak peaking up above that perfectly aligned forehead of hers was graced with delicate, soft, cornbread, creamy skin. Her cheekbones were so high, an *American Top Model* scout approached her once at Cosi's salad fast food buffet and pleaded with her in earnest efforts to take the application. He, in his high-heeled white Baby Phat, affordable crocodile thigh-high boots, Affirm relaxed tresses splayed in the perfecto Mohawk/dreadlock and pink British imported lipcake that did well to hinder his ashy coffee without milk or crème complexion, at first glance knew Ms. Tyra and that damn lush everyone wished Omarosa woulda knocked out on that Sur-*Rich Losers R Us* reality show already, would be impressed to the point of complimentary emotional tear jerking praise just before a suiting and appropriate CoverGirl commercial.

But A.M.T.BB Jones or A'phrod'item'ta'beebee'Jo Jones (as she preferred to be called but, we shall call her Ms. Jones for the sake of time), did not desire such a lifestyle. After all, she spent most of her weekdays watching ABC soaps even though she frowned upon such cushy, my-parents-are-rich-so-I-do-not-have-to-work-at-Burger King-type of bitches. The characters, in her eyes, were ungodly, too skinny, wore too much makeup on a daily basis and--quite frankly--not the type that could handle theyselves if they man or woman ever got caught up and locked up fa not being a mutha-bleep-bleepin' snitch.

But it *was* fun to watch soaps as her six-inch nails dried from their four coats of clear, spray paint protecting polish. So she prayed to Jesus for forgiveness after each and every episode.

Now, even though she found herself tired of saying thank you to numerous male admirers at the Highland Park strip mall she visited on a daily weekday basis to window shop and add items onto her Rainbow fashions and Footlocker wish list after the ABC soaps and her favorite court shows went off, even with all her male admirers, she had a serious man problem.

See, there was this one dude, Rocka-Shady-Puffin' Rhymes…and *man* was he *fine* with his pimped out platinum, white gold and cloudy diamonds straight from the Discount Expo only "two hun'ed fa uh cluster" grills that he changed on a daily basis. I mean, the dude had one for each day, and sometimes, if you looked really, really closely, you'd notice he had certain grills painted with special retainer/car rim shining lacquer. How could any girl resist such a thing?

But that wasn't all.

He had buff shoulders that made him look like some sort of steroid god. Thank goodness he spent five years in prison cause he "ain't wanna sell out" his mama "fa getting her hustle on at da mall wit dem fake credit cards lil' ManMan had hooked ha ass up wit," he had four self-done tattoos from the cell time as well (and shid!--that was sumen ta be proud of cause he ain't even have shit ta numb hisself wit, as he always proclaimed before pulling out his gat fa sho on niggs dat didn't know who *he was* up in da club). To top it all off, he had gone to Job Corps and was currently working on him uh associates degree. In liberal arts. Fifth year now.

Ms. Jones liked that--an educated man.

Maybe he would one day get a city job. You know, when his hustle got knocked by cop'pa's who didn't have shit bedda ta do than bother hustlas in da hood--Ms. Jones could get all political on that shit. Hell. What was wrong wit uh brotha selling uh lil' sumen sumen ta cousin Keisha if cousin Keisha liked ta git high? Whad da fuck was Sista Souljah smokin' when she talked about niggas selling mess ta they own? Humph! That was how money was made and laid in her hood; that was how Escalades rolled down the streets all smooth and quiet—kinda like Ms. Jones demeanor.

So she got to thinking, as she sat there skipping her daily Rainbow/Footlocker weekday routine, a prayer was in order. She prayed over and over. And as she prayed, she stroked her fake diamond necklace from *Chima Hee' Da Neegas Cum* Chinese beauty supply that specialized in African American beauty products and knock off Vuitton purses that hurt the eyes miles away because of their bright, fake, thick, sweat shop leather glaze. The necklace hung all the way down to her waist. She was very, very proud of that necklace. It *almost l*ooked real. And, shit, I'll be darned if Nelly had one on at the Grammy's! She loved Nelly. He looked like he could be Rocka Shady Puffin' Rhymes long lost cuz. She prayed so long, she almost missed the pork chop dinner Big Ma had cooked. She prayed so long, the family mutt, Pepper, that kept opening the gate to their backyard and making herself at home until Big Ma finally said she could stay and made her a part of the family--that dog started calling out to her from underneath her window.

"Oh, Ms. Jones. You have been kind to me over the years. You once gave me your pork chops the time you went Muslim after watching Malcolm X. You once took me to get my flee issue disinfected. You even got me spaded after you noticed how mean the street kids were to my pups after they begged you to let them take them home. Oh, Ms, Jones. You are kind. And for your kindness, I shall repay you! I shall repay you!" The golden brown mutt danced in a circle. The same kind of dance she did after someone threw her a few good scraps of pigs feet out the window during a Sunday family dinner.

"But you are a dog. And I know I ain't lost my doggone mind. You ain't s'pose ta talk." Ms. Jones was confused and flat out scared. Maybe she'd drunk too much Boones Farm earlier that morning? And maybe she should have held back on the forty ounce she shared with Auntie Nessy when she had come over to celebrate her fifty-dollar lotto winning…hmmm?

But this was no time to wonder. What was this damn dog on?

"Pepper. You are my favorite pet. But silly thang! Dogs not s'pose ta talk. I'ma ignore yo' ass, sweetie. Shid. Lemme pull out ma bible and pray—sweet Jesus." Her voice reached an all time, wavy sopranic high on the last *s* in Jesu*s* that lingered in the air like crickets hissing throughout a long, sweltering summer's night.
"Oh, no. You needn't fear me, Ms. Jones. I would really like to help you. I *would*, I tell you."

"*Help me*? S*illyd*og!" She said the last two words so fast and so country, they blended together in a singsong fashion. "I thought I was drunk but maybe it's *yo' ass* we need ta worry 'bout," she finished.

"Well…then…forget it." Pepper began walking away from underneath the window to her shed that was tucked far away in the backyard dirt. There was no grass. Only mud or dirt depending on the day, although Big Ma had done well to make a garden of tri colored flowers in the front. Big Ma had a crush on Rufus, the red-boned, fifty something mailman with the thinly lined up mustache and the bad case of razor bumps. And he truly adored her Marigolds, Black Eyed Susans and Carnations. Sometimes he even plucked some of the mint sprouts that grew on the side of Big Ma's house and chewed on them. Good thing he'd never seen Pepper ease herself over there. And Big Ma never told him, either. When he'd choose a mint sprout, she'd simply place her hands on the sides of her stomach un-hidden in her lavender and white moo moo and chuckle.

"Pepper. Say what's up or walk yo' ass on ova ta that shed, B." Ms. Jones was becoming irritated. She had other things to do. Like go get her lashes done by Marvelus the Tranvestite on Seven Mile. Or she could hit up Joe, the white nerdy guy who taught at the city college and secretly liked Black girls and had a panty hose fetish. He liked to dress in lingerie and shake his butt like the girls in Ludicris's video *Pussy Poppin'*. She hated to watch but Joe always gave Ms. Jones money for it. Sometimes even two hundred dollars when she let him wear and keep her Victoria Secrets Barely There bras. For thirty minutes of chicken skin poppin', who could argue that she had not earned her weekly hair and nail money. She went to church every Sunday with a clear conscience. It wasn't like she had done anything with him. All she did was watch. She had ta make her money, *what*!

The dog snapped her out of her private thoughts. "Never mind then, Afrotransvestite." Pepper began to walk away.

"It's Aphro*dite*—APHRO*DITE*! *DI-TE,* you buzzard! I ain't no man!"
Pepper continued to walk to her raggedy, paint-chipping shed. For some reason, Black folks just did not seem to care about their beloved pets in the same manner as White folks. This was the reason there were so many strays in urban cities. Just looking at her shed made her depressed. She wanted to be inside where the air conditioner was. But Big Ma had deemed her too dirty and flea prone to be in a house full of young children. There was a total of ten kids in that house. How they all fit was still a mystery to Pepper.

"Wait! Wait, pepper. What's up? What's the dealy-o? How you gon' help'me?"
"…W*eeellll,*" Pepper's voice had taken on a Peppy La Pew kind of accent. "If you really want to get that Rocka Shady Puffin' Rhymes you've been sweating like a bad case of the flu, all you need is a bigger butt—and." She brushed at the nails on her left front paw, "I can help you get it," she added.
"My butt ain't flat! What'chu—"

"--Do you want 'im or what, Ms. J?" Pepper interrupted.
"Well sure! But! But!--"
"--*Butt* is what you don't have." The way Pepper accented it made it sound almost like a criminal act. Like a felony. "Okay. Simply close your eyes, rub your butt for five minutes and imagine the letter C while doing so. Then, you will have your rump! That is what Rocka Shady Puffin' Rhymes likes. He does not care about brains, he does not care about face or looks for that matter—I guess that was why he last hooked up with the mixed thing that had that terrible receding hairline just before he went to jail for—"
"—Pepper? Pepper! I do not care to hear about Whiggerlina! Just tell me what I need to do ta get his fine ass!"
"Yes, yes. I see. As I was saying, he does not care about anything but the bum-bum. So follow the procedure I just told you and you will be fine. Wait for him outside Footlocker tomorrow. He should be yours."
"Thank you! Thank you Pepper! This evening, I'ma throw you some extra bones—I promise."
"Oh, no Hon. Just a warm sudsy flea bath would be nice, thanks."
"Aright, aright. Flea bath it is."
"Cool. See you and your new bum later, darling."
"Um-hmm. Fa sho." So there she stood, in front of her newly purchased Garden City Furniture mirror Big Ma'd purchased after cousin Keisha's four year old little girl Ralaylay had climbed up on the old antique dresser Big Ma's mother had put in the will just for Big Ma. Ralaylay had banged her head so viciously against it that it broke in half. She was the epitome of a crack baby and had a seriously uncurable case of A.D.D. No one even dared to whoop her. Besides, the new dresser was nice with its simulated wooden drawers and plastic mirror, so Ms. Jones had no complaints about Ralaylay breaking the antique one.
"A butt, God. Gimme a C-lookin' butt. Make it so big, a nig could sit a glass on it while I walked 'round da club." She smiled envisioning herself looking even grander with a big ole, Sir Mix A Lot butt. Nice, juicy, brown and round. "A butt God, a butt. A big ole', big ole butt. Aww," she sung.

And Pepper was on point. Just like that, her butt was rounder, much more firmer, less J-LO jiggle-o and looked like something Serena would envy! Truly envy!

"Thank you, thank you Pep," Ms. Jones said after running out of the house to head over to her favorite hangout/wishlist spot. She had no time to kiss all the babies on her way out as was her usual custom. None of their fathers or mother ever came to visit them since they were either locked up, on that white rock or "gone to a better place" as Big Ma liked to put it. So all ten of them called Big Ma, Auntie Nessy and Ms. Jones "Ma'Da".

She was so excited about her new proportions, she didn't even ask before taking Big Ma's brand new STS. She just rolled out. Usually she walked the three block run. But today was special.

As soon as she got to the US Cellular, bullet proofed Walgreens, Cash Advance, Sure-Tel phone service, Chima Hee Da' Neegas Cum beauty supply, the Arabic owned grocery store that specialized in carrying nation-wide generic foods brands like Americas Worst and Heartyfull Hazards, the Rainbow Everything Under Twenty Dollar Store, the Footlocker, the Moo and Oink and the soon to be shut down for Osha violations Coney Island that was now successfully running going out of business specials and causing a new influx of stomach flu to circulate the greater Detroit area filled strip mall, laden with jitneys and begging male bums no older than twenty, she parked Big Ma's brand new purple Caddy and jumped out of the car. She'd even switched her pants to a fitted mock velvet, jogging number that showed off her new item. As always, she stroked her almost real, tarnishing diamond-like necklace and popped her Apple flavored gum so loud everybody knew she'd arrived as she sucked on her 'soon to be gum' blue Blow Pop simultaneously.

Immediately, as though it were kismet, Rocka Shady Puffin' Rhymes turned around. Even if his smelling faculties were shut down, he'd be able to smell booty coming his way.

"Whad up, though, Ma?" He smiled his pimped-out, cloudy smile her way. She eagerly soaked it up, popping her gum louder with satisfaction. He'd finally noticed her!

"So...what's up?" she asked still playing with the necklace that was certainly responsible for the green ring now hovering around her neck. But her butt was big. And he didn't notice the green. Besides, green was his favorite color. The same color as his freshly painted hooptie. And his contacts from Chima Hee Da' Neegas Cum's beauty supply. And the C-notes in his pockets. Rumor had it, he drunk so much of that green 251 proof, he often left a green ring around his main girl's toilet bowl.

They went back and forth with the "whassup" for almost fifteen minutes before Rocka Shady Puffin' Rhymes grabbed her new buttocks and kissed her so hard her lips hurt and she swallowed the green wad of gum.

"You my new main girl," he stated smiling that shiny smile. Ms. Jones smiled a greenish blue smile back. She was so happy, she couldn't balance her head. It bobbled back and forth—sort've like Beyonce in "Bills, Bills, Bills".

And so it was. And she, Ms. Jones, was almost happy.

She did not return to Big Ma's house that night. Instead, she joined R.S.P.R. at the spot: his house that doubled as a drug shop.

And because her butt was so big, he even shut down all the traffic and moved his business elsewhere—he had respect for his main girl, huh!

Now *that* made her truly happy. And Ms. Jones in turn, cooked him grand meals—just like the ones she'd never helped Big Ma prepare. She helped him do his class homework—so what if she had to do it all for him because he couldn't read; she loved her man and would do anything for him.

But after three months passed, she noticed he was staying out in the streets longer and longer. He'd shoot dice and shoot anyone that contradicted his win. He'd eat at the Coney Islands that ignored the city ordinance and still served drive thru from behind the boarded up windows low-key cause they still had five more relatives to bring over from Saudi Arabia and didn't quite have the money yet. Even though Ms. Jones would skip her favorite court shows to fix him five course soul food meals, he just didn't seem interested anymore.

And it wasn't like he was cheating. He was a Taurus sun, Capricorn moon, Virgo ascendant with a venus in Cancer for heaven's sake! No cheating going on here! But something just wasn't right.

So, after much deliberation, she made a decision. She was sure. She was positive. Her butt simply wasn't big enough.

That night, after he ignored her love note text messages, she did exactly what she had done months before to get the glorious buttocks that had won her her thug. That had to be it.

For years—three to be exact—she had tried to garner his attention. She'd done everything shy of hula hooping at the strip mall with the elementary school girls out on summer break and still hadn't even gotten so much as a glancing over. But with this new butt she'd made her way into the crib and had even shut down the previous hussy.

And so she did it. Her butt measurements granted her a whopping forty-three inches in circumference measurements.

And just like that, her man was home the next evening. They watched *Jeopardy* and *Wheel of Fortune* together before heading upstairs to the bedroom where they spend five hours. Four and a half of those hours Ms. Jones spent making her butt clap for R.S.P.R. and, although she was tired from all that cheek shaking and clapping and had slept the rest of the day, everything was good. Just as good as before. Even better, maybe.

That is until a week later. When Mr. Rocka Shady Puffin' Rhymes decided he'd rather hit the Greektown casino. And seriously, Ms. Jones tried not to be mad. She was after all part Greek, right? But it simply became too much to bear! He *never* came home!

So. She had no choice. She had to get an even bigger, better, GRANDER buttomockous! That was all to it, goddammit!

She stroked, she rubbed, she sung to that butt, she made it clap. And after three hours, girlfriend had four—not two—four butt cheeks! Four of them bad boys! As hard as it was to imagine, it was true. The mirror was not lying. Four. And it was not such a nice thing! Even she was disgusted with her new bodily attachments. She looked like she had an ape hanging on to her back. It was even hairy! Like a deep, dark, auburn dyed floor length mink! It dragged and lagged behind her. "Her ass! So disgusting and such a pitiful sight to see. It's not even the same color as the rest of her body!" Detroit eastsiders would exclaim each time she stepped foot out of the house.

Easily she became a recluse. The house was a much safer haven. But even then, although she was now always at home, the house turned into a sty. She could not get up or walk around for longer than three minutes without falling short of breath and having to take another break. Her butt. It was simply too GRANDE! With all the similarity of an extremely, extremely tall Starbucks Latte loaded with much too much sugar, given to a midget patron for the killing--heart disease, heart murmur, kidney failure, diabetes, high cholesterol—all shortly entering his life from just one latte. For Ms. Aphrodite Marsusala Tamiky Blessed-Be Jones, the four flaps of her buttocks now threatened a similar fate. But she could not bear to reverse the process. If R.S.P.R just came home, surely! Surely! He'd see her butt in all its heavy grandness and would only love her more. He'd love her more--dammit!

But Rocka Shady Puffin' Rhymes never came back. Rumor had it he'd hooked back up with Whiggerlina who looked like a White man with a big butt. But Whiggerlina was really a woman, though.

Ms. Jones wanted to be a lady about it so bad. She really did. She couldn't bare the high of being with R.S.P.R. only to fall hard--a serious downfall for her flapping ass loaded with four compartments. She couldn't take it. She popped up to Rocka Shady Puffin' Rhymes newly acquired westside home. But he wasn't with Whiggerlina either.
"I thought yo' ass hooked up wit her." Ms. Jones asked/stated.
R.S.P.R. laughed. "Nah." He shook his freshly tapered and smooth brown shaven head. Without the bottom and upper grill, he looked like an Ambercrombie Fitch type of dude.
"So you just up and leave, Rocka? I loved-ed you!" She couldn't contain the fervor in her chest.
"It be's like dat sometimes, sho-tay. Yo' ass was tryin' too damn hard. Shid, if I woulda wanted a dog, I woulda bought one."
"What?"
"I said if I woulda wanted—"
"I heard you the first time! Wait a minute! I was tryin' ta make you happy, Rocka Shady Puffin' Rhymes! I did everything fa you!"
"I know. I know. But I 'ont know. It was jus way too much. When you went ta class fa me and offered ta do ma time in jail fa me that was it. I couldn't take it no mo'."
"But I—" she started but, he interrupted her by placing a finger over her now quivering lips.
"I guess this was a lesson you was supposed ta learn, sho-tay. It's all good. I still got mad love fa yo as—" he coughed to cover up the unfitting word choice. Ms. Jones folds were situated against the sidewalk with great awkwardness. They shivered against each other in the chilly evening air giving a rippling wave effect. "I still have mad love fa you ma but, I think I need ta be by myself fa uh'while." he turned and walked up the single, solitary cement stair of his ranch aluminum styled box shaped house. It looked almost too small for him as he squeezed into the tin foil looking screen door. Watching him disappear Ms. Jones felt weird. She wanted to be mad, but somehow couldn't be. Instead, she bought herself a forty-ounce and headed back to the house they once shared.

After numerous hours, she managed to reverse the damage she'd done to her rear end.

Later that night on television, there was Dr. Rey, that 90210 surgeon, talking to some saucer-lip-looking plastic surgery addict. She began laughing but then stopped. Had she not have been able to reverse the booty situation, she too would have been a talk show freak.

She decided to go back to Big Ma's.

Everyone was furious. Once Big Ma confirmed that she hadn't been kidnapped or killed, she smacked her so hard, had she not been able to reverse her four booty cheeks, that smack sure would have!

All the kids were pissed part of their "Ma'Da" had been gone and Auntie Nessy couldn't handle all the kids by herself and had moved to Canada plus she needed the Canadian healthcare anyway.

Even Pepper was slightly cold towards Ms. Jones. "You were plain greedy and selfish. I would not have helped you had I known you would paraded that big butt around and totally turned your back on the very people who loved you. Did you know that Big Ma had to walk all those kids to daycare on her amputated foot? The poor woman was limping and hobbling about. It was truly a sad sight to behold."

Ms. Jones leaned down next to Pepper. "Look Pep. I'm sorry. Really. But I've been thru enough already. Seriously. Things got so bad I couldn't even walk for longer than three minutes without having to take a nap. I've learned my lesson."
Pepper rolled her eyes.
"I'm just fine the way I am and I don't have to sell myself on anyone. Either they will accept me or they won't," Ms. Jones insisted.
"Yeah. But one bit of advice."

"What Pep?"

"That necklace is going to give you gangrene of the throat if you don't take it off."

"Pep." Aphrodite Marsusala Tamiky Blessed-Be Jones put her arm around the dog's collar. "Thank you." With that she got up and went inside to help Big Ma fix dinner.

9.

speaking of transmigration, the whole process is free and legal

this—this book, or whatever this self-appointed author has chosen
to call herself—is something. Something to read when drunk.
...or,
maybe for one who has become sad and is looking for something
that does not really matter

to ease their favorite fear

and in such a case
please do not read #3 and some of the others

and in such a case
the author (ha! *whatever* the chick thinks she is)
would sincerely like to say:

fill in your own wish and do remember
words have atoms
and even if you don't
or cannot speak
or simply do not wish
to say hello,
do fly without wings
and find yourself in

------------- place

or

------------- on vacation

or

------------ (   )

when life becomes Blue
and Blue has become your only friend
or else
Blue will move himself in and, though he's cute
and swishy and lays very comfortable between your neck and your pillow,
you may never be yourself again,
unless, like the author—or whatever the freak calls herself—he is

your favorite color…

10.

The End

At rise: A sunny day on at Lake Michigan, Pete and Evelyn sit on Pete's yacht...

Pete
Hi Honey it's--

Evelyn
--Don't call me honey, you fuckin' bastard!

Pete
Okay...alright. Evelyn I didn't ask you to join me today for an argument. I simply just wanted to see how you were doing. The kids said you have been taking everything kind of hard and—

Evelyn
--The kids? The kids? Oh, now you've become Dear Ole Daddy. Funny how you barely even talked to them before.

Pete
They're my children too, Evelyn, whether you like it or not--

Evelyn
--Whether *I* like it or not? If memory serves me correct, and it always does, you dear, sweet dear ole dad, never even came to one graduation! Not Tommy's, not Tina's and not even Tonya's and she—*she* was your favorite!

Pete
I had to work! We had bills!

Evelyn
Hmph! You were too busy picking up boy toys to remember your own damn kids! The ones you begged me to have! Left—

Pete
--Evelyn! Please. Would you just calm—

Evelyn
--You, dear *slut*, have nothing to say to me right now! I flat out hate you! There, I said it. Shoulda said it a few years after the I Do's were in order. I shoulda left you after I got my ring and access to the checking account! Hmph! Made me wait a year! And I really loved your ass!

Pete
Go ahead! Go ahead! Since you obviously need to vent, I'll let you--

Evelyn
--huh! You'll *let* me? *Let me*? Let me tell your ass something. Since I was eighteen it's been all about you and what you want! Peter wants dinner at six, Peter's had a bad day, time to give Peter a massage. Oh, it's not a good time for me to go to college right now because Peter needs me at home. Peter's career. Peter's new car. Will Peter Please buy one for me? Will Peter give me a good allowance this week? Will Peter even show up in the labor room this time?

Pete
Come on, it wasn't like that and you know it. You're just angry.

Evelyn
Ya think! You, you actually brought a *book* to *read* while I was in the labor room delivering Tommy! And guess what? Guess what? When you went to Italy for three months back in 1986, you shut the joint bank account down and didn't think I'd be smart enough to contact the bank and figure it out since your all the *'Good Ole Boys'* worked there! I had to use shampoo to wash the dishes! *Shampoo*! While you were over in Italian country clubs or whatever the hell you were doing! Me, personally? I'm glad we're divorced! I finally have a chance to live!

Pete

Good! Maybe you'll stop being so angry then. I would like to eventually be friends--

Evelyn

--Friends? Fuck you! Turn this boat around! I'm ready to go home.

Peter

Evelyn. I know I did some things—some terrible things to you and the kids but…I didn't bring you here to argue. I—I thought you were cheating on me! I didn't want you to be giving that Georg guy or whatever the hell his name was, the money *I* worked so *hard* to get! I--

Evelyn

--You nothing. Oh, yes. One more thing: about your lil lover boy, Mason? FYI: …*Set up*! I paid him to hook up with you, get you to fall in *looove* with him, as you now so eagerly claim you are—and voila! Peter-free. You made me sign the prenump, right? So, now, we, my dear, are even.

Peter

You what? You? What? Mason? No! It couldn't be possible!

Evelyn

Not so fast.

Peter

Give me the gun, Evelyn.

Evelyn

For two years Pete. Isn't that about right? I would know--that's how long I've been paying him!

Peter

You're just trying to anger me! You're just trying to anger me, right? ...

Evelyn

No seriously... Peter! Peter! Oh, my God. Now people are going to think I pushed him over the boat! What am I going to do! Helpppp! Helppp!

11.

The Check N' Go

Here is Albert Fanning.
Chocking back wet, soppy, hot tears American male style as they should not cry. Mad because of a back left-side molar.

It rotted two years ago but the brother was so disregarding, and, really, the tooth wasn't hurting, so he just moved on. It even turned a frightening, orangish-gray around the gum line. And started withering into corrosion. His excuse—he was a full-time student; he didn't have time to waste in some brand new hotshot's dental office.

Truth be told, he was flunking out of college as fast as pimps get ran out of heaven and he was about to start at the new chic-salad place that served leafy greens in olive oil and oriental concoctions that were more pretty to look at than healthy. Yeah, he was going to be a "Will that complete your dinning experience?" plastered smile appeaser for a whopping nine an hour. And. That was better. Better than nothing. And better than five measly, nincompute somethings per long dreary, leg-cramping-inflicting hours at that costume shop and being teased by passerby's with Village People songs when he clocked out.

But back to this here tooth.

So now the boy is laying in bed all day, twitching in pain, over one nerve in that tooth inflicting pain in such a way, he is beginning to believe the tooth to be the person or entity behind all human suffering and injustice.

But he must do many things today. Like go pay his Verizon bill lest they cut him off from communications with other human spirits and the female sirens he later wishes to shove parts of himself he can justifiably acclaim without shame to be eight inches, into future would-be dates.

And, then too, he has to go see his grandma of whom has lost her sight in such a way, she has come to believe him to be Prince. (At first that was fun, singing "Purple Rain" and "1999"…but, over time, as with anything else overdone and overplayed, he began to resent the theatrics and her constant demands—"Sing it again! Do it again!" over and over again from the time Judge Mathis went off until Girlfriends came on four hours later. He felt like some kind of eighty-year old casino entertainer still woefully emulating Elvis.

But back to the tooth cause I know you're wondering what the tooth has got to do with all or any of this.

Yeah. The tooth. Because he'd been behind on a car payment after giving this really hot Nephertitti lookin' chick who'd started working in the gas station next to his apartment a really nice gift for her birthday—a *Madea's Family Reunion* DVD along with a gift certificate to the Rainforest Café (with the hopes that she would invite him to enjoy it with her and to her place afterwards—which would mean an eight inched debut) because he had been low on funds, he made a trip down to the Check N' Go in that brand new plaza they'd just built that looked just like all the other ones in every other city in every other state belonging to the United States.

The Check N' Go.

He pulled up, in his brand new Infinity embarrassed to go in. He was making payments on a payment now some four months later. But hell, people had bills, right? He wasn't any different. So what if he never made it past happy b-day with that damn Nefertitti girl. Black females always said they wanted good brothas but never seemed to recognize one when he popped up right underneath their noses. Nefertitti, in all her head wrap, lock wearing glory, was now dating some punk ass gangsta who could be found rapping ever Sunday at the Catholic church at 9 o'clock morning mass, twelve o'clock at St. Peter's Episcopal and Baptist Heartwarming and, last but definitely not least at the Bad Life lounge on Crystal Lake Drive come eleven o'clock pm. Silly girl. At least *he* could offer her free salads come lunchtime. All *that* dude could offer were spectacle shows every Sunday!

When he slid open the Check N' Go doors, the tired bell announcing his presence rung and made his ear sting and his back molar tooth throb a whole lot more. And the cigarette smoke the white haired, gravely voice had just conjured up out of his noise annoyed him more than his present life lot
"She'll help you, Albert." Yes this greyhound dog-looking guy knew him by name. Four months and still paying, remember?
"Okay." What could he do but say that?
"Hi you," she spat out in telltale cigar smoking fashion. She sounded like she was a hundred already but, Albert Fanning decided she was actually somewhere in her late forties.

She was the type his nightmares were made of. The stiff, uniformed curling iron inflicted dented curls that made her look like Sister Bear of the Berenstain Bears. Those god-awful burgundy, oval shaped press on nails. The lipstick that matched and did not fully cover her lips. Like she was embarrassed of the size of her lips or something.

But what really did it for him was when she smiled. Only three teeth on top. Was Check N' Go that f-ing desperate? What had happened to this sista? Where was her shame? When he made his $20 payment, she spread her lips so wide, he wanted to fall in from embarrassment for her.

Hadn't his mother said something about AmeriPlan the other day? Didn't they offer discounts or something?

"Hey, I just forgot. My bad, ma'am. I need to take that twenty back."
"You whud?"
He didn't have time to think he just grabbed it. It *was* his money!

Two doors down was a strip mall dentist. The kind with the big, tooth outlined in blue in wired lighting with a yellow smile pointing at the phone number.

12.

A bad incident

I know this is gonna sound weird but I don't have anyone else to tell all this to. My mouth, it's getting out of hand. I've got this one wisdom tooth on the left side at the bottom. You should see it. It looks like a gigantic piece of ivory. Definitely not like a human tooth--that's for sure. More like something stolen off a baby elephant. It's growing too big because of this theory I've figured out.

See, four years ago I did a stupid marriage stunt that I was innocent enough to think was gonna last. Problem was, both of us had been way too sheltered by well meaning, yet stifling parents who'd done everything the devil wanted them to do but were determined to keep us from reveling in just a few ounces of similar pleasures.

The minute we said the "I Do's" we both started wiling out. That's what happens when you've been repressed for twenty years. It mighta been cool if we woulda hung out together every once in a while—after the marriage I mean. But I was "eccentric" and he was a-ten-trick. Word at his job was he'd hooked up with every ten-dollar hoe in the city when he was out in the field on jobs. He worked for the water board and at the mall and trust me when I say he'll be seventy with a walker and still digging in holes in the daytime and asking what color towels you preferred on the weekends.

It was really quite embarrassing. Not that he was a hard worker--not that part of it. It was just that he'd pick the most very wrongest moment to blurt out that he'd got drunk at work again and had a tussle with some guy who'd knocked over his Coney Island smothered pork chop dinner and then had to go to anger management for three different workshops that totaled up to four months. We'd be out with a seemingly nice couple. They, for instance, would be talking about a trip they were planning to go on--Australia or something of the sort and here he'd go blurting it out like he was a Desert Storm Vet still coping with flashbacks. "NOT ME! I AIN'T GETTING' ON NO PLANE! AIN'T NEVA BEEN ON ONE--AIN'T 'BOUTA GET ON ONE! SOMEN 'BOUT DEM THANGS JUS AIN'T RIGHT." Then he'd turn to the guy and say, after giving him an ole punch-a-roo in the shoulder, "But man, you shoulda seen these rats that was bitin' on my work shoes yesterday. I was in dat hole fa eight hours straight and they ain't let up. I got three holes in my shoe ta show foe it! But I 'on't wear dem no where but work, though." At least that was the truth--thankfully he didn't. Already on the honeymoon I had a problem getting him in the shower. That would be our fight for the following three years. That and the daily brushing of his teeth.

And herein lies the rub. As one could probably surmise, he had no respect for health management and such things humans with easy access to modern civilized contraptions now deemed necessities this day and age...well, except for that one time his triflin' ass had caught himself a good case of Chlamydia and tried to blame it all on me. We hadn't even been around each other for more than a few months since I'd put his ass out for driving down the block with my arm stuck in the window of the car my mother had given me. He rolled the window up and I hadn't grabbed my arm quick enough; I couldn't do anything but run down the block with the car and hope the tires didn't catch my feet.

He was mad. I was always late and making him late and even though we had another car—a brand new one that his genius father told him to lease--it was currently well over the mileage limits and was sitting shiny and still in the garage. Since he had been gone, I knew it wasn't me. But he went around telling everybody at church that I, his wife, had given him that crap. Now for that, he *did* go to a doctor. But what difference does it make when you continue messin' with rat bitches who only like you because you make $12.16 an hour?

Not even a few months later, he was in trouble with the church for letting his bestfriend's pregnant girlfriend live in this burned up pad he was living in for $300 a month. He was cheap like that. I remember that one time I went there with my bat in tow to find him so I could beat him down for talkin' shit. That house was five different colors of peeling paint. Red, white, blue, gray green—you pick a color. Well, when I caught him off guard pulling into his driveway (I had parked my car in his backyard and was contemplating on breaking all the windows and driving off but I wasn't sure if the crack dealers and their crackhead partiers next door would notice) I leaped inside the minute he opened the door and peeped the forlorn state of his living status. A wall about to burst in from water damage and a completely burned-up upstairs. The conditions were so bad I forgave him for letting the human she-rodent live with him. Besides. The guy who'd rented the place to him was related to the kid who the pregnant thang my 'supposed to be spouse' was going with at the time and they were pissed and he was about to get kicked out of church until he proved that he had repented. He needed somewhere to live. Why not come home? And his skin tasted good; like dark, cherry flavored brotha.

All over again.
The arguments. The constant not going to sleep for fear of what the other one might do while the other one was sleeping. It was very not good living like that, in fear of the worse half. That's when the bags under my eyes started, the suicide thoughts wouldn't stop rolling in, cheap wine was a nice friend and police calls were nothing awful or new.

One argument: health insurance. There were good choices but he just didn't care. Why go to a doctor with a co-pay when you could just go to the Wellness plan that was one great leap away from Medicaid? That's what he was used to. So what if some of the nurses didn't know how to find your vein and so what if you had to wait an hour even though you were on time and so what if the doctors had rashes all over their faces and scalp. It was free goddammmmmit!

So my solution for all this nonsense was: switch the health care myself and I started going to the dental school. I wasn't about to go to the same dentist he and his family had been going to. You'd have to see his family's teeth to understand why not.

I had gone to the dental school when I was a kid for braces. My dad had looked over my teeth one day before announcing to mom that braces were definitely in order (thanks dad!).

But this time the dental school was different. The walls weren't shades of dark indigo blue and crepe papery looking and the lights weren't silvery and recessed and didn't hide the smudges of fluoride treatments rubbed around your mouth so that the boy that would be cute one day soon once released from a two year headgear sentence couldn't see how ashy from fluoride your face was.

The only thing going on there were people that looked like they were in multitudes of pain and couldn't afford any other alternatives.

All the students had thin, sheer arms and forceful fingers that sometimes shot you in the tongue instead of the gum.

After the first one, some weird boy left, I got a girl who was cool and had nice skin. But between the boy and her, they both fucked up my tooth at the bottom. She, the girl wannabe dentist, kept convincing me that I had a cavity or 'carry' as she called it. I didn't see it. It wasn't bothering me. Already she had convinced me to let her pull two of my wisdom teeth. She got me on a vain tip. "It'll mess with you orthodontic work," that's what she said. Later on and $300 after the fact, I found out from a dentist who refused to remove the other two I'd been convinced needed to go as well, that she'd just needed the credits.

But this chic was good at convincing. I was driving back every other week to get the 'new carry' fixed. Five different times. One time she dug a hole so big she had to overfill it with that silvery mess that taste like mercury and then I couldn't bite on anything for a whole week.

Then the filling fell out and since you're probably wishing I would speed up this awful, awful story no one really cares to hear, I had to go to that dentist at the mall that his—the ex—whole family went to.

A dentist at the mall. How contrived is that? Just doesn't sit right, does it? In and out in an hour… And then, to top that off, I came in about the tooth I couldn't bite down on and here he was, this meaty fingered Arabic dude trying to extract my leftover wisdom teeth without even asking me! I jumped up after he sawed down the tooth that looked like a cane sticking out of my mouth, screamed at my ex but then hubsand the whole ride home and kept running my tongue over the sanded down spot. Felt like a tree stump in the mouth.

A month later, I was chewing on something—a McDonald's Big Mac and a little silver thing clinked onto my tongue. Every week a little more silver crumbled off.

Two years later I was grabbing a bite to eat on campus and *bam*! A pain that felt just as bad as when the ex had dropped me to the floor head first that one time I came home late, surged thru my mouth and forehead. Damn tooth.

A year later I noticed my face becoming real fat. Nothing else, just my face. Then the headaches started. Then one day I was doing my routine in the tub praying underwater about all the stupid things I had done to date and, although I got out the tub feeling refreshed and sin-free, I couldn't hear for shit. Then I couldn't eat. Then I couldn't sleep. Then I noticed the big ass hole in my mouth.

Now that me and Mr. Hole Digger finally got the divorce we both deserved but could have worked out and now that I don't have dental insurance and have to walk around repeating the same mantra I repeated during our marriage and our regular fights and after the end of that gorgeously awful marriage, "It doesn't really hurt, this pain is not real," all day like a dim witted guru and every time I go to the dentist they look up my history and call his people to see if I am still on his shit and then they start talking and trying to figure out all the reasons we are not together because someone at his job is always eager to relay some part of the story and I end up hating the fact that the government can get all up in your personal like that. Why don't they just ask me if I mind if they call his insurance people so I can tell them, "Hell to-the-muthuafuckin' *yes*, I mind!"

Who knew life could be so miserable over one little small thing inside the mouth? Me.
I'd gotten comfortable. No more pain. Generic Vicodens were good cover-ups.

Then, I go out of town to meet this dude I never should have met. He had the same name as my most recent ex who I later decided to quit denying was slow…(I wonder if I am slow since I chose not to believe him to be slow…? Hmm). One thing me and my girls have discussed and come to a reasonable conclusion on is this: never date a guy who has the same name as your ex. I have three friends that have done it and none of the outcomes have turned out good or even mildly okay. Bad ex experience? Leave all others with the same name alone. Trust me. I might seem a little crazy but I know what I'm talking about when I speak on things like these. If it is a good ex-experience (which I cannot imagine because why would you be exes, then? Unless someone moved away or something and even so, now there's internet and webcams) I can't help you on that one. The good ex experience is out of my realms of expertise.

Which leads me to my whole point.

I didn't even like the dude. Just like at first when I didn't like my ex with his same name. But he (the new and already ex 'experience'—'cause he wasn't a boyfriend) kept pressing. And he said all the things a girl wants to hear. "You need someone. Sometimes it's nice to talk to someone when you're all alone." And I was all like, "Not me! I'm good." And he was all, "Don't give me that I don't need a man mess!"

And voilà! There I was rethinking my position and checking my scheduled flight on my email even though I am an expert on knowing when a guy is not right for me. Actually, I guess you could say I am an expert on knowing that a guy is not good for me or that I am not good for him and still going right on with it like somehow we are going to become right for each other. So *that*--knowing better but doing it anyway--is another thing I can add to my lists of expertise.

But I mean really. Who wouldn't want to go out of town especially if they hate the town they're stuck in? No he wasn't that cute but…well. It was something to do. Although when I think about it, I had plenty to do as it was. Homework, cable television, work, eating mangoes, a few dreams to think about at 4 in the morning when I can't go back to sleep and the heater keeps creaking like a stomach ach and a hangover that is about to hurl any minute, music to play loud enough for the neighbors to bang on the ceiling like a bunch of whoot-a-nannies--plenty.

But here I was out of town (don't wanna say where in case someone in the know should one day read this which I really and truly hope does not occur. Then, what would be the purpose of me telling this story right now? If I had someone to tell, I wouldn't be doing this and in that case this is now a total waste of time!).

*** (Now I am mad. This whole thing is a waste of time. Just like my out of town trip and just like my first sexual experience and my first and a half marriages. A waste. And I don't even feel like telling you the rest. But I *will* say this:

Even if you don't like someone, sometimes as a woman you feel obligated to have sex with them. Yes, I know it shouldn't be like that but when Hugh Hefner is still a pimp and bragging about Viagra and has young hot chicks crying over him and wishing he would just settle his wrinkly ass down and Snoop can take two chicks to an award ceremony on leashes, although I'd like to consider myself a neo-free-ist and all-woman-empowerer, amongst other things like educated and neat and funny when I am not worried about my teeth, I sometimes fall victim too. I, at times, have been prey to perfect June Cleaver and a society that enslaves women routinely.

And shit, I hadn't had any for 4 months. Sometimes that is just the thing that'll get a bitch caught up ((I find it pertinent to add here that I am also sometimes ghetto. I used to mind, saying that I am that—ghetto--and all but now I realize it is just a word as with anything else. And in that case, these are just words and although they—as I have stated a few times before—are a total waste of my time now, how do you really know if this whole thing is real or if I just made it up so that I wouldn't have to listen to my heater throw up again before I fall asleep?))

Anyway, after too many shots of Patro'n and after realizing that I *did* want to get to know this guy a little better and he was ignoring me which I hate, I ended up in the hotel letting him stuff his face with my second set of lips afterwards requesting I suck the tip of his thing. He liked that. And we went to sleep hugging, which was a very nice change of pace from the way I have been sleeping—on one saggy pillow with another one tucked in the crease of my empty elbow.

I was okay with it after that. Well. Not really but I can't tell you why. And not for lack of words either. I know the reason. I just do not wish to tell you.

Once I came home everything was also okay but not really. I was watching the final episode of *Flavor of Love* and then everything took a turn for the worse. I went to the bathroom--it's always something with me and bathrooms nowadays. The doggone tooth started hurting when I got in the tub, remember? Now this. I decided to brush my teeth—had eaten too many sweets. It's close to Halloween you know. Candy is everywhere just like the rain here.

But I open my mouth real wide to check up on that tooth that is in deep trouble until I get my coverage next month and low and behold what do I see. A mouth titty! A mouth titty on the side of my poor, abused tooth.

And who do you tell some shit like that to?

So I started thinking and worrying and worrying and thinking. And that's when I came to this theory: Got to be sperm.

I got a mouth full of sperm incubating in my gums! Sperm!

Now a guy that I don't even can't even say I like, a guy that I don't even think likes me and always says he's on the other line when I call but calls me when I don't expect it, a guy that I know for sure I'm not supposed to be with, I got his sperm growing in my mouth--a whole lot of *sperm* growing in *a hole* in my *mouth*!

I took a q-tip and squeezed as much as I could out. Yep. It was squishy like what I suspect sperm takes the shape of after a week or so.

Well…that *was* my theory until my girl Co-tan (fake name just in case she reads this) called and I told her this whole thing.

She says it's an abscess.

13.

Death Does Not Part Us

If you have ever wondered if the day would come when women were treated as part of the human race rather than second rate slaves only capable of serving men, it has.

Year 2160.

Imagine women not having to wear suits or look male to be in corporate offices. Imagine opening up a Jet magazine and seeing a man in a thong, commercials for jock itch and low sperm count, a man begging his woman to take him back even though *she* cheated and is now in love with another, men always displaying their sex in movies and on ads for everything. Imagine men talking about love in raps, men called trifling for leaving their children behind, imagine women being revered for carrying babies for nine whole months, seven out of ten men being raped, women not having their clits cut off for purity and tradition, a woman getting some without being labeled a hoe and if, unfortunately, a woman and man split, people would wonder what is wrong with the man rather than whisper that "something's wrong with a woman when she's attractive and can't keep a man," Imagine a time on earth when a man doesn't treat every other woman he comes in contact with terribly because one woman many, many years ago broke his heart.

Imagine mothers being paid more than strippers, imagine phone sex for women with men telling them they are beautiful every ten seconds, male cheerleaders for the WNBA, imagine the WNBA being just as important as the NBA, imagine God having a wife and that Jesus is their son, the bible telling men to be good and quiet and helpers too, imagine a queen having more husbands than King David. Imagine love finally being taken as seriously as being on time for a job interview has always been.

Imagine.

Keep imagining because in December 31, 2159 every human, man and woman, was killed.

When the Splegitariecs came down to earth they treated human women so kindly, every human woman decided (which took a lot of effort because human women had a history of never sticking together on anything—sort of like Black people after the Civil Rights Movement) to leave earth and go with them to a spot next to Mars across from Wakensnewly/by. They'd have to wear permanent stars that would encase their entire bodies from the strength of the sun but they were fine with that. Splegitariecs men were so deep and kind they could seep thru their star bubbles and reach the soul of a human woman as easy as it is to eat two orders of Rally's/Checkers fries.

They'd never seen anything so divine as a human woman. On their planet there was no such thing as the opposite sex. That was just the way it had always been.

But when the Splegitariecs were taking the human women into their bows and arrows (that's how they fly—in bows and arrows) the human men went into unanimous uproar.

So the Splegitariecs said as it was their way, "Let us be fair."
"Okay," the human men replied in the usual earthly male accordance.
"Treat the women better than we are more than capable of doing and we shall all go our way in acceptance of defeat. Three days we shall give you. From our location next to Mars we will observe everything, however, we give you our word, we will not intrude. We shall only check the status of your situation five minutes after ten o'clock AM and seven past seven PM human time. If during those times our findings determine you clearly not upholding respectable treatment and all that is kind toward your feminine counterparts, if we should see the manner in which you deal with them is inferior to what we willingly offer them, then, the women, if they wish, can leave with us when the first starlight hits the vicinity of your upward horizon.

In the background the women objected. All the human women shouted angrily, "We wish to come now!"

"No. No. We the Splegitariecs cannot take you away from your home without giving your human men fair first opportunity. Already they have seen what happened to China without women."

"Okay," the human men agreed and the minute the Splegitariecs bowed and arrowed into the air and then into thin nothingness, they, all the human men on earth, turned to all the women of all the lands of earth's entirety. "We would rather be without women than forced to worship them!"

The human women saw the looks in the eyes of the human men, the entire mass of them, and knew they could not physically over take them.

"We're men. We don't have to worship you women!" all the men in the US agreed. The Canadian men "Here, here'd."

Hyacinth Houston-Rice, an ancestor of Whitney Houston and Condoleezza, knew what this meant. If Canadian men agreed with the Kuwaiti and the Chinese and the American men, all the women on earth were doomed.

Ms. Houston-Rice decided to try and reason with their simple egos. "The Splegitariecs are not asking you to worship us. They have merely challenged you to treat us better than they are more than willing to. We wanted to leave but you were not happy with our decision..." Hyacinth withheld all emotion.

"No! Why would we treat women the way *those* punk ass bastards did! Be nice to women for what? Y'all ain't shit and we ain't goin' for that. Y'all were put on earth to help us and do what we tell you to do! We're *men*! Y'all ain't shit but the weaker sex!" an American man shouted.

At that, all the human men of every land, from every country on this here earth ran toward all the female humans, the girls, the toddlers, the teens, the mothers; mothers suckling their newborn, older women who smelled of garlic and onions—all things considered female and human and they killed them with their bare hands choking and crushing in necks and female skulls. Pushing and weaving feminine souls into the deepness of the plush earth, an earth unwilling to accepting them alive. They grinded the hearts of women until they were distilled into red wined water dripping into browned over soil. Once mixed with the dirt, the blood of the women turned earth's terrain into cement; hard, filled with holes and unpromising.

"Ah-ha! Hail be onto man! Hail be onto us! Men rule the earth!" Howard Stern's great grandson to the twenty-fourth power, Howard Stern XXIV declared minutes later over the still shaking and soon to be rotting female bodies peppering the earth.

When the Splegitariecs looked down at exactly seven after seven they could not believe what was in the focus of their vision. To make sure their sightings were accurate, they quickly arranged a meeting and declared war, dressing themselves in silver Kit-Kat wrappers—Armors of Declaration is what they called their Kit-Kat militia robes (we would not like to go into further detail as to exactly what the Splegitariecs look like because we'd like nothing more than for you, the reader, to draw your own conclusion (which is just a nice way of saying that their looks do not really matter. They are nice. Nice men).

"This is our world and we don't want you on it!" the men yelled riled up to fight with the Splegitariecs who'd just arrived.
"You actually think that we care take great heed of your wants? We do not care what any of you want. We made concessions with you of which you agreed yet you did not honor the treaty you signed."
"So tha fuck what! We're *men*! We don't have to honor shit!"
"So you'd all rather be dead than to have women by your side if it meant respecting them and treating them as your rightful equals?" the Splegitariecs asked.
"Hell yeah! Women were put on earth to serve us! To serve *us*! You can't have two captains on a ship!" All the human men cheered after one man from Istanbul responded.
"Dere were no problems man, til dey sent dem tings down fa da Adum, if you don' kno, da by-ble tell you dat one, hey-man," a Jamaican shouted bolting his mug of beer into the air.

"This is how you really feel?" a Splegitariec with a hand located on top of his shoulders in place of a head (fifty-percent of them are created in this manner) questioned, finally understanding just how alien he was to human man.
"That and the rest of it!" a British man replied and with that the Splegitariecs blew into the air and demolished all the human men.

To this day the Splegitariecs send glass stars down in remembrance of the once lovely humans ladies who existed years yore and had changed their lives the moment they'd come down to earth to visit. Life would have been so much more wonderful in their location next to Mars with human women there to share sun clippings and water shines and golden brushetta.

14.

crazy neighbors

Every night he does this. At the same time.

The father runs downstairs naked for reasons only he knows. His family, the wife, the two girls and the middle child, the boy all hide so they don't have to see him. It is like watching people scramble down the escalator for a train that has already departed.

The house is big enough. There are many places to hide. Rooms, rooms and more rooms. Some have hardwood floors that shine unapologetically, some have carpet in colors like muted mauve, lime green and willowed crème. The living room is one fourth of the downstairs. It has the hardwood, mauve drapes and white curtains that billow softly in the night like there is goodness all around. There are light fixtures hanging heavy along the walls but no one notices; the room stays dark; light only comes from the moon all silvery sweet and ominous and it makes things appear beautifully scary. There is only one picture hanging in there—a painting of some lady dressed in a white dress of old trimmed in blue lace with an umbrella in a forest. She is White with loosely pulled back blonde hair; the family is Black. Then there is a den. It, too, has hardwood floors and a small, screened-in back porch and a stereo with a record player lives on porch along with the first daughter. She likes to do her hair in the mirror she's leaned against a windowsill out there and more often than not she chooses to listen to the cars zip by instead of the stereo. Next to the porch is a half bathroom that smells very awful, like too many spoiled bottles of Lysol, a kitchen that is brown and yellow and depressing with it's own back porch of which is very untidy and filled with old newspapers stacked up past the windows that no one will ever end up reading, a dining room off from the kitchen that is decidedly boring but big. An entrance that does little to promise anything of the house's many surprises, a coat closet that is stuffed with socks and pens and green florescent paint, stairs that amazingly are not broken and chipped from all the running…

Upstairs is amazing though. There are rooms that open into more. Sometimes parties with famous people hanging around and tons of servers dressed in their black and white uniforms lined up waiting for the next thing to happen as it always does. There are bathrooms with sunlit slots and teal green walls. In one room in particular it is always semi dark. The television is always on but the screen is always blank. The carpet changes up on you. Sometimes shaggy, sometimes flat and uncomfortable like cement. But the thing about this room is, there is a lady that always wears a fleece hat who is always adopting kids. And there are tons of kids. They move in and out of doors and closets preoccupied with fixing their lunches for school and they go unnoticed.

There is another room that should bother everyone. It is dingy, the walls are burned black and money green. People lay around on the floor. Sometimes it is vacant except for the dead lady with the bun on top of her head. She isn't morphing into dust like most things of old do. She just lays in that bed in the bedroom right next to the white kitchen with the light teal green and white tiled floor and the second story back porch everyone goes in and out of.

There is another place deep down below in the house. It is underneath the basement and that lady with the dark curly hair from that one television sitcom lives down there. It is very dark with only one light in the whole place. When you come in you are scared at first but once you past the living room with it's metal kitchen table straight up from the fifties and teal vinyl looking chairs you can slide right off if you don't like the dinner she's ordered that night, the kitchen is rather nice but doesn't have a table or other trappings of the living room and there is a bedroom around the corner that is warm and full of dark wooden furniture and cream drapes and sunlight and good memories.

And you can fly into cities and touch the tops of the buildings across from Parks and lakes--but only at night. Sometimes you can look right into people's windows and see what they are doing at three in the morning. Some college students are studying, one girl is communicating with her friend on another floor thru a

Styrofoam cup muffling their words back and forth. The words flit and fly and bounce off all the plastic things in their rooms. Girl A is mad because her boyfriend is ignoring her and she secretly wonders if Girl B is hanging out with him at that very moment. Some people are boxing up things because they are being evicted. Some places are empty unlike this house.

Everything is shaky and uncertain.

One day you are in the old neighborhood on your way to first grade and the houses look skinnier than ever before which is very uncomforting but when it's all said and done and you are not flying anymore, you want to return but you cannot justify why you must go back. You have a crazy craving to go back to those exact strange patches of land with white skies and small houses that should be motor homes but aren't, back to places where people gather in arenas every evening and listen to preachers preach under orange spotlights and watch football competitions and swimming jumps for God at the other end of the stage…

Somewhere far, far off there is a block where the children skid along the street real fast and real slow on their bellies on brown and thick yellow striped ski slopes; they only stop on red lights. Their destinations are always one of the two restaurants in this city/house: the one that is always empty and almost dark with amber lighting and brown waitresses that look Asian and wear their black hair in various ponytail fashions…with bangs, sometimes without; or the restaurant that stays packed just because of its name and the hotel rooms that look over the dining room and the man-made river that flows throughout the first floor. This is a much better view than the projects around the corner three blocks south of Zero street. No one wants to live on Zero. In fact, they are planning to do major gentrification on that street. Zero. Then everyone will want to live on street Zero and the people already living on it will know they were put out and misplaced for a good reason.

If it is a forest that you wish to walk thru then you are fresh out of luck. This house has many things but a forest with tons of trees and animals that are furry and cuddly and predatory it does not have and really, it is not such a shame. There is enough going on as it is.

It is not that this family is an ignorant bunch, rather, they are too consumed with their own daily affairs to notice all the action and all the Light Beings who live with them. But tonight they are waking up.

The oldest daughter, Shiloh, is in her mirror in the den porch again. It's her hair once again this time. It's all gooey and gross. Her locks didn't turn out right. It looks as though she has a package of greenish-gray clay swirled into a beehive on top of her head. Some of the locks have fused with the rest of her hair and because she put too much product on her locks, her whole head is now a hot mess. She is scared and thinking about shaving all of it completely off. But then what would she be? She is already not so cute looking.

The father zips down the stairs again, naked and singing. It is undecided as to whether or not he is angry.

"Ugh!" The brother Timmy shouts and slams himself into the half bath that smells like rotten Lysol.

Shiloh does not have time to hide which, this time, is actually a very good thing. Not the seeing your parent naked part--the fact that she was around part.

The father didn't go anywhere once he rushed downstairs. He just stood in the living room behind the couch. There was something in his hand that he was tinkering with. A light flickered past and it didn't look like the traditional car zooming by. The horizontal blinds covering the window in the den rocked back and forth. Shiloh could see it in the mirror. Then there was a flash.

Shiloh is scared about only one thing—her hair. Upon witnessing this strangeness going on in the window, she walked right over and pushed the blinds back. There was a man peeping in the window with a crowd standing behind him. Now maybe he'd heard about all the things going on in this crazy house or maybe he had something for the dad during his late night runs—who will ever know? But Shiloh called to the rest of the family and they all stared at the people who were leaning in and looking inside their house thru the window. The people standing outside were looking at them the way people lean and look over caskets at large, much anticipated funerals.

"Who are they?" the mother asked, her voice shaking.
Timmy ran back into the bathroom his knees moving like the mother's voice.
Stacey just stood with darting eyes looking from her father to her mother to Shiloh.
"What do you want!" Shiloh shouted aggressively.
The man tried to rush away. You'd have to be on a ladder to stand up in the window like that from outside but he wasn't on a ladder and that was weird. Somehow he had hopped up there and was perched on the ledge. Shiloh opened the window and pulled him in.
"I said what the fuck are you doing!" she shouted. But really she hadn't.
The man stared at the gleaming hardwood floor wanting to say that the shine on the floor was very impressive but he decided at the last minute not to say it.

"Well. This is what *I* think." Shiloh went into the kitchen and got a butcher knife.
"No," the father interjected.
Instead the mother knocked off the man's head with a piece of the wood trim that was hanging from the doorway that led to the kitchen.

The man's head bumped against the white tee shirt he was wearing before falling onto the floor and the family went upstairs and got in bed and headed off to sleep and the father never ran around the house without clothes on again and the mother continues to knit with her eyes closed (Kita and Dwinnie are not always over because they are doing their own thing with their own husbands and kids like they should be doing and honestly, after all these years, 25 to be exact, they are tired of telling her to stop—she likes eye closing so much she won't stop anyway) and the father loves his wife enough to wear her eyeless creations.

15.

Lady Martyr

I could sit on this stump
and play victim for you.
You would like that. Then they would say,
"She was very sweet. He should have kept her." Or not.

Yes,
I have always been the bad girl
even before you bit off pieces of my heart
and slowly chomped and chewed
until it turned this syringed blue hue.

At least bad girls
can be their own recovery therapist;
I am not a bright bitty ball of woe
or angry or another romantic tragedy

I am not even lost anymore
still thinking you are the final
destination.

At least I am not in your bed
cranking new found friends
dipped in 151 proof
until finally cut off at the pulse.

I am happy not being restricted
and bound to gangrene,
backwards hypocrisy.

Now I smile
and look into the mirror
and count the unremorseful
pleasures that have run in and out
of the electric thunbergia

hidden in me like amethyst thunder
and I am not reminded of your wrinkly balls.

16.

scab

i have scratched off my surface
i have tried to be like them
perms are a monthly affair and when they say,
"Whut up ma nigga?"
i so easily pretend not to care
and continue hiding my queenly flair
scared bone hair straight of the one word:

                       Weird.

It is nothing like fake hair
--that sort of labeling
can't just be ripped away
and takes years to repair

now accustomed
to the pus running wound
i keep pulling at the scab,
pulling at the screeny scab
more repulsive each day,
this sell-out tab.

17.

mrs. saint

She had her own issues,
secrets all neatly wrapped in an abundant ball and lodged in the back of her throat.

Never drunk nothing but Kool-Aid, Pepsi and Christian Brothers, lived in undercover motels $21 for 6 hours when she was 19, dressed her daughters in shoes two sizes suffocatingly too small for fear they'd one day grow past 7's and 'cause that's the only size the booster had that day, she dyed her hair red, threw on the gold ankle bracelets and ignited the Blind Pigs in the Black Bottom on Hastings.

She had her issues,
secrets all molded with the fuzzy white circles, tucked and locked in her stomach.

Hated the light-skinneded chicks with "good haya," refused the dark dudes with hair like hers—even after the moonshine and the nickel bags and it all paid off cause her babies was pretty but boy did she beat them toddlers for walking too slow down the side walk.

She had her own issues,
secrets all hustled and patted securely in her bosom for safe keeping,

like the three years the children raised themselves while she clutched a new nigga tighter and when the school bus arrived who had time? Shid, she was sleeping thru that damn 60's revolution that was making sistas let they hair go bad; who was a Nikki Giovanni? Who gave a fuck 'bout somebody's LeRoy Jones? Put dem Temptations on, let the records play and keep her only real lover-friend, that liquid stuff heroin, uh rollin'!

She had her own issues,
secrets all in all

Now the saint, dipped in the cloth of the lamb, preaching at the pulpit, imbedding those tiny black words on tissues of white paper, licking each page during The Sermon with unpolished nails, trying to inculcate those holy, holy words into the sheep that left the devil outside,

condemning and singing, singing and condemning—dancing is now out of the question—hurting those not listening to these new words of her tongue with promises of pitch forks and blazes that will never stop, her tongue is the measuring ruler of right and wrong.

She corners me at the end of all the commotion. She wishes to discuss the ailing spirit hovering over me… I failed to Amen and Say It Say It on the inches and centimeters of her tongue.

The saint wants to heal this devil.

18.

bored

it is January 6.
i am bored to tear drops.

to
counting the lines
of the hardwood floor

to
keeping the company
of the boy with the big
stomach with three kids

to
watching the clocks
green hands move each minute

to
counting calls
on the caller ID

to
listening to the man upstairs
snore and snore and choke
and snore

to
looking outside
and checking on my car

to
watching the man
ring 3's buzzer

to
cutting the pubic hairs

to
writing evil—famine
and all sort of overalls—
a letter
diffused in hate

to listening
to the pounding earache

to
laughing
at nothing quite loud

to
making up a song
about galloping cars

to
actually liking
the friendly faucet drops

to
blinking my eyes
to find that yellow spackle
of light

to
practicing facial exercises

to
actually sending the letter to all true evil—
famine and any sort of overalls
to an address

bored to the point of…

19.

prison

Ohh,
I am locked into the cruelty of infatuation. I wish to greedily swallow your smooth, moist lips to spare the earth of their beauty.

In one satiated gulp your sensuality would be all mine to glow within the embers of my stomach. Even with a lipless face void of your divine pout, I would then be captured by your delightfully happy eyes that laugh and glimmer inside those willowy lashes.

Your steady walk, unexplainable quietness—how can I bear inside the prison your lickable caramel whipped skin has imposed upon me?

20.

on strike

Did I scare you with my upfront, I want to know you better approach?
When I asked, you looked like a zebra too close to this lion. I am truly sorry. This time you were in person rather than the main attraction in another libido raising dream. I got excited.

You said yes. Reliably kept your word. During that time I almost lost a shoe, produced enough facial oil to fry catfish for a family of ten, said things definitely inaudible and acted a bit uninterested. The lion sometimes melts into a hairless rabbit.

Your fake smile that now greets me on our occasional run-ins (I must stop her to reiterate that I am not quite a stalker) lets me know the dream has faded.

So it is, now, that my heart, my mind, feet and hands have gone on strike. My legs have gotten to the point of feeling itchy with a burning sensation—the way one feels after running without a good warm-up while wearing pants too tight for a good run.

I am prepared to picket all night on top of the frosty needles of grass in front of your house…

It would be nice if you would one night peek out to see me.

21.

crumbleton: and the crumbs that follow

I sit and cry at the kitchen table. These crumbs can never be put back together. Once their hearts have been broken, they will never be whole again.

They are so stubborn, these crumbs. They stack on top of each other still refusing to come together, to form a whole piece like the way they were before they got crushed by someone or something or a plump finger.

All they do is scatter. And they are not fun to watch because crumbs are very boring and no one cares about them. They just get wiped away and are garbage bound.

I am still sitting at the kitchen table.

No matter how hard I try they are still crumbs, minuscule pieces of what they used to be. Not even leftovers are so bad.

22.

Special K

Your name stays branded in my mind and, just like your face, it is beautiful symbolic graffiti that I cannot understand all over my thoughts.

I have these redundant dreams in a distant dreary city and state. We live in a strange, bi-level house. I wear the sexiest navy blue, fitted Chanel suit with the cutest navy crystal buttons, a 1930's hat with a black feather in front toppling a pageboy (to trick the unsuspecting foes) with the skinniest, pointiest Manolo Blahniks. You wear your favorite jeans, black tee shirts and those cute black and tan bowling shoes that are now in style.

We have discussions that satisfy each synaptic knob in the brain and protect each other in the racist, oppressive elements that continually saturate us with women taking their clothes off for money without giving them proper respect for such things. You don't necessarily like the way I infiltrate the sexist infrastructures surrounding us but you accept and love me and never try to change me. That is why I am only comfortable with you. Your embrace is the kindest thing at the end of my long hard work days. There are other people there that I have liked (like Morris Chestnut and Pharrel and Tavis Smiley) but not as much as you. In these dreams you do everything right—like not unremittingly gazing at other girls when we go out. You care beneath the make-up and the monetary gain for me. And you are friends with the other person who lives inside me. Our blood types even match.

After a few weeks free from the nuisance of your addictive intrusions, I'll be functioning in my own lil okee-dokee life on the freeway coming home from school. But as usual, your face pops up on newly planted traffic lights. You then you again on the red and the green and I almost run into a Mac truck doing 90.

You are starting to come in many different forms:

mannequins, friends, neighbors, movies, models then yourself again. Just when I think the fantastic exciting nightmares have ended, you sprawl into me months later and double-dutch all over my thoughts. This excavation of the mind gives me headaches. I even purchased a book to decode these things. But I took it back. I should have never let you in that one time you didn't have anywhere to go.

Three steps to the big, four steps to the small as I walk down the dream erasing hall, flakes of you all over the long graffiti scribbled wall.

Let's make a truce since (in real life) these fantasies have no use. Be kind. Turn me loose.

I let you go and turn the corner.

Pe-pee-peek-a-boo! Guess who?

But of course,

It's still you!

3:4 pain ratio

23.

thank you

Thank you
for making me lose weight.

Our thin crust, nightly pizza sessions were really beginning to take their toll. And being drunk, debauched Baileys and Grey Goose style was not always so cute in the morning. My head would still be caught in between the sheets, between your legs and I was nowhere near chemistry class and or the punch clock--paid internships are hard to find...

Only recently
--you know,
when you insisted I meet your family—
then called it off right after--
it has become fashionably difficult to eat.
Thanks to you I can now wear a 0.

P.S.
The exact same shade of red as my eyes,
the sign that sits above the instructor's podium and reads:
    Fire

    Fire

makes me throw up.

Yours Truly,

The Person Unwillingly Remaining A Hot Gluttonous Desire For You

24.

Untouchable

Mersega, Mersega,

You are just as beautifully unclear as your name. You float in the dead leaves of fall phantoms and swim place to place in warm, kissable summer heats.

No one knows where you go,
no one understands your next move. Fluid you are, like purpled, sand colored chiffon scarves dancing in the wind, never still.

Your wide open eyes are always frightened like captured doe each time we move in closer to see you and your sparkling chrysanthemum toes.

Mersega,
many of the lands most handsome men and even the prince himself have asked for your hand. Whether or not you are barren of Fertility's kisses, they would only find delight in your russet spiced tendrils, your golden twinkling beauty and ruby, sugar filled lips yet you float away into your cactus filled desert like dust unsettled.

We have invited you over for gossip and mandarin tea but you seem to prefer your own shadowy brew instead. Will you ever invite us to its rich secrets?

Mersega,
So untouchable, torturing us with intriguing stories of a life held deep within your cherry-blonde, scorching coffee eyes. You are the phantom that encompasses our lives.

25.

a writers revenge

I hate her. That thing should not even be categorized female. Looking at her is like watching a 49 year old person get potty trained for the very first time.

Ms. Du Pre,
licking off sugar walls. Wanting us to join in and help you suck your very own clitoral balls.

Do you do illegal substances Ms. Do Do Dupre? Cause you look like you fall a lot and your dazzling nose job now sinks in. Now you look like a fluke Ms. Duping Du Pre.

26.

new generation

Sitting in the auditorium on a bench on the bleachers there is Fya, pronounced Fie-uh, like someone with an east coast accent trying to say fire. Fya does not look happy or pretty like she used to when I knew her back in high school. Even back then she had sad eyes that held secrets of waking up and dressing all her sisters for school, feeding them salami sandwiches each night and never knowing when she'd see her mother or father next. Even then guys found her attractive. Today, years later in this unknown time, her lips stick out like a fish gasping for water. Her once wavy black hair is now dust filled tangles—the kind that come from years of not caring.

There is a baby next to her that, oddly enough, looks as old as Fya now does. Chunky, he wobbles like a spinning top toy. He is undoubtly hers. I name him Catfish Baby. He has a chin that, I am sure, holds a beard. She is not watching him as he wobbles along the bench. It looks like he will not get that far anyway. And her mother is at the end of the bench. She never introduces me, still, I know the lady with her hair slicked smoothly to the back, the lady who looks more like she could be Fya's sister instead, who is holding her head high and barely blinking as her eyes are affixed on the happenings of the stage, is her mother.

"Aw, what a cute lil' boy," Fya boringly remarks about the eleven year old on stage raping. He is jumping across the stage like a fruit fly. At what I am hoping will be the end, he turns around and shows his back to a mostly indifferent and chatty audience. It looks as though he is struggling with his buckle and at that very moment I know I do not want to see what is about to occur. I turn my head and shield my eyes. When I am finally brave enough to look, he has left the stage and an older man is sweeping the small brown turd off the stage. The old man shakes his head and moves out of the way for the next act.

27.

oh pretty one

You are so pretty,
a cute, small button nose,
how does one breathe?
Perfect hair, perfect eyes.
…Perfect.

For you dear pretty
we will name a star and maybe even wrap some around your head.
we will let you slide on traffic violations and be Simon Says until the pretty wears off.

Once you are older
--say 14 or so—
we will give you the privilege card and ask you—no, beg you—
to become our million dollar Super/Uber-baby so everyone can truly appreciate your beauty. Your face will be on commercials and on every common girl's *Seventeen* stash.

Shortly thereafter,
a huge billboard displaying your youthful breasts and hardened nipples will intoxicate the eyes and earn the lust of old married men (how else will we get them to buy this stuff for their wives?).

You will smile on late night shows using given words of our choice
and you will dine in the finest restaurants the world should offer.
You will have your choice of liqueurs and delicacies some will never know.
For you are pretty and deserve the best!

Now if you should cry for one second, for any reason at all,
we will wipe all the stains away with the ungrateful broom and shush you back
to your pretty little world.

There are worse things that could happen:
uglyfatpoverty and no more Koreans to sell their hair, no more manufacturers to make designer bronzers, Dooney and Burke going out of business…

No, no. We could not bare that.

28.

the way of the world

"On the real tip, the bitch isn't *that* pretty--she's not pretty at all. But she thank she's cute. I hate females like that."
"Yeah, look at how long her arms are!"
"Ugh, yeah. They're way too long for her body. Turn the page."
"Ooooh. That's that new singer. He is *sooo* hot. I have to watch his video like every time it comes on 106 & Park."
"I know. He's a lil bit stuck up—don't you just love it? When a guy's real cocky?"
"I know, even if the guy's not all that cute, when he's cocky it makes him *wayyy* more hotter."

29.

rant 1:
therapy <secret code: wo/a/c>

Look. I am so sick of this, people always getting everything twisted. I am not going to explain myself. Yes, I've made mistakes—plenty: talked too much at the wrong times, opened up to everything wrong and, because I always get what I want, I get bored and chose the wrong man to love so as to create a challenge and sometimes people think I am slow because I am dramatic and sometimes loud and this lady at one of my old jobs actually told me indirectly that she thought I was retarded so I used her mistake to my advantaged and fucked up shit on purpose—if I were slow I would not be able to help fucking shit up, right? and even though I played the game and had fun doing so, I hate when people try to hint instead of using tact and being direct and, it's not like they are fooling someone, you still know they're trying to diss you in some strange way and it only makes you dislike them more and wish they'd taken a Dispute Resolution class which, I myself just did so I wouldn't have to always be ready to use my stun gun and my new pink and silver revolver and my neighbors think I am doing something illegal and why would I care since I am not and I know the wife is putting pressure on the hubby to make him hate me and get me kicked out and I think it is because I am helplessly sexy even though I have finally grown up and toned some of it down so that I look a little more serious and so that I will not be at the library in clear heels and she—wifey--is way too pale and chubby with a bad curly perm and although I hate to talk about people and to hurt people's feelings even though I can sometimes be mean, I do not always wish to be but she will never know because she keeps having phone conversations about the fact that she has never seen me without makeup like it is her responsibility to see me makeup-less and this person she is on the phone with must be someone else equally as boring and with as much time to waste as she herself has and the plain looking hubby that you would not remember if you saw him at Wal-Greens, works for the FBI supposedly and sometimes I hear the wife call the blonde haired police friend of theirs and police guy enters the building and tries to pretend he is not trying to investigate me and one time they put a grotesquely plastic plant with ceramic bulbs the color of a whole color palette next to my door on a white spray painted wicker stool so I moved the witchy looking wicker thing to another spot in our building so they would understand that sexy chicks are not always stupid--they must have thought I was pretty dim in the attic to put it there and think I would not notice and I even checked other floors and did not see such grotesque contraptions victimizing anyone else's doorway and this (although it hasn't really) has made an excellent segway into another thought that has crossed my mind which is that I am tired of people that hate rich people and stuck up people; life would be much better if everyone worried themselves with how to be the better whoever they are's before they die and why do people hate people based on hear-say and rumors? I can understand if they have had a personal experience with the person and decide they do not like them based on their own conclusions but I do not understand those who merely live off the impressions of others and how come we are letting all those people die? For them this war marks the end of their world and I wish people would think about this sort of thing—every day Armageddon--instead of me. Maybe we are smaller than atoms, maybe we are smaller than see-thru faeries some think are make believe even though they keep hiding everyone's keys, maybe we are not even made up of matter because matter really matters and so many of us trapped on this here beautifully sweet and bitter planet act as though we do not.

4:4 pain ratio

30.

what the cat ate

You are what the cat ate.
Yes it's true
and now I'm all pumped up in hate
wishing I would have gone to that seminar late
so I wouldn't have ever ran
into you and your Calvin Klein suit

Ooh,
I so hate you
you did every thing you could possibly do
to make me give up pork
and mayonnaise loaded cheeseburgers
and my dreams of New York

just
for:
you.

Then you flipped the switch
like friends on Judge Joe Brown.
Look at how you got my head spinning around!
I should have known
in love there's always an infectingly severe glitch
and it's always worse
than calling your mother a smothering and controlling bitch

I so hate you
and I'm glad we're thru
you're the thing
I'll never, never again do
worse than Kelis, I hate, I hate, I *hate* you!

You are what the cat ate.
Yes, it's true
...and now I'm all pumped up in hate
wishing I would have gone to that seminar late
so I wouldn't have ever ran
into you and your cologne...
You should have just left me the fuck, fuck, fuck alone!

Ohh,
I so hate you
you did everything a person could possibly do:
calling every day just to say hey,
sending tickets Hawaii
any time the written words went sad,
understanding different isn't always bad,
playing the Roots CD with the poem at the end
'bout the girl with the set-up 'cause you know I like it when the women win.

...And the buzzards buzz their own lil' twirping, twiddly-twoo songs--I know, I know, this has nothing to do with anything right here but in life, sometimes something that has nothing to do with anything just comes along and jumps right in just like this...

You are what the cat ate
--another swarmy thing in the sea
not meant for me,
a false cognate,
the thing seeping thru my belief
love today then a thing of the past,
making me wonder if anything good
ever lasts,
the thing turning my heart
into excavated tunnels
like empty wells.
the thing turning my eyes
into lifeless silver bells.

Yes,
I will once again
wear that mask
and no one will never,
ever know the real, real me
for no one really cares to see

…all y'all damn fish in the sea
not one single one ever cared about me.

31.

for rant 1:
something

I dream in record players that stood like music towers and called my name when I first began to crawl, in sienna fields filled with people stuck inside for a reason, in memories of Farmer Jack on Warren near Woodward long, long ago when you could dance in the Ice Cream Isle # 12, in fat women that always brought over something fried on Fridays, in a house that hid TV and pulled out plays before toys, in odd wooden benches with odd songs sung for the lord and carpet-like gray chairs, in talk radio played at night before the jazz hour, in sleeping next to a-used-to-be-friend that counted how many times the guy I wanted looked my way that day, in men with wide brim hats and trench coats on Lafayette street before it went gutter, in houses that look like boxes but smell of jasmine, in an old lady I call grandma while others call her Muh who took me to school with her when I could not talk and almost lost her job because mother could not afford day care… in walking with mom to sell Avon, in riding to kindergarden on a bike because we had no car after the blue throw- back Monte Carlo one burned up with me in it, in daddy's tenants coming to the house banging on our doors, I dream in fear of nothing except having to leave behind favorite perfumes in airplane terminals, I dream in colors, in the happiness that comes from controlling your own world, in teardrops that store million dollar promises unknown to the crier, in blasts that go off each time mother of the land of the dark gets stung and raped and the commercials announce bling with no dark owners to profit, in fights every Friday that hurt but no longer, in a friend I call dad, in an uncle that is always there at 3 am for the good date/ bad date details, in not needing anything but closed eyes to be happy, in good deodorant to look out for me when I get too hot, in lips that do not need lipstick, in a tongue that can make you happy, in arms and hands that are strong and keep trying when the mind is weak, in finally learning to be and in learning to let good come to me, in being okay with being two or three contrasts, in a particular man just for me who lives in New

York and calls my name in a way all his own with that cute east coast accent and his weed smoking lips so soft it's a shame and in the way he kisses my forehead after we play the touching game…

32.

(no title)

Should I ever get a dog, I will name her or him Marmaduke.

Or maybe ShaLaylie. Or Taffy. Or No-No. Because these are cool names. Why else?

And dogs are sweet. They are loyal no matter how mean you are to them and they are always looking forward to seeing you when you come home from wherever you have been all day. And they listen when you talk and they do not sit in windowsills like cats choose to do even when you ask them to stop. Yeah, dogs are nothing like cats nor people. You can't trust anything in either one of those two categories—not even yourself if you are human.

Or maybe Sarah is just the name for the dog I might one day get. Sarah: because lately no one has been using that name and the Sarah's of the world are disappearing.

Or.

Choncha. Because one time in D.C. I saw that on a menu and wondered more about it and I would want people to wonder about my dog. That way if she or he is sick, someone will come to visit him or her or send a card—because they cared enough to wonder.

Or. Love. Or Good Thing. Because words are loaded with power and I am sure my dog would be a nice, nice pet.

Silly Goose is not such a nice name though, for a dog. Now if someone wants to get a pet giraffe that might be a good name.

...I wonder how I can get a pet giraffe. They are nice and do not make as much noise as dogs named Miracle and Bullet Toe and Buffy the Vampire Slayer Television Show. And I definitely think a giraffe will keep the thieves away. Can you imagine? Breaking in a house to hit a lick and seeing a giraffe? ...*Exactly*.

33.

electra paradox

"I want my ankle back!" Each time she exclaimed it her lavender rose colored eyes dropped a trek of glimmering tears onto the ground as though it were the first time. But it wasn't the first time, it was the 95th time all ready. On 7th street, New York, New York, zipcode 10018. And when you looked down at that one lonely thickened rounded off leg nub, you could see the rust growing more scandalous night by night. When she tapped on it ever so lightly, she'd fly right next to the moon to that town we have never decided to be Wakensnewby or Wakensnewly just yet. But there was some sort of hold up. Steela told me it was the space up there—way too much for catching one solitary little ankle and foot.

But I know the real reason. The reason she puts on so much.

It's not that ankle she wants nor needs so badly. It's the baubles. Those shiny, pretty, made for three more lives on Wakensnewly/by baubles.

There are iridescent dangly silver diamonds so sheer they are wonderful places for hide and go seek. The bands on those baby's are transparent diamond crystals only these are credit, rent and money free and they grant youth good for 300 human years.

It's not the ankle. No-sir-ree-bob-uh-dee. It's not even about the money--that lady is already loaded.

It's about that charm bracelet up there dangling in the sky as if it is the only real living thing in the whole world.

That ankle called me yesterday on my cell. My cell is so bootleg I almost couldn't make out who it was but that ankle has a very distinctive androgynous squeaky voice that is undeniable so I figured it out. Even when it tries to prank your phone you know the voice is that of Ankle—(Recently Ankle quit using its phone because it said it hates the way earth government officials taps the lines and stuff). Anyway, Ankle said space in Wakensnewby is way too much fun. Maybe I'll go tomorrow to see. The ankle says it's better than Hawaii. I can't imagine that. How can anything be better than the Virgin Islands or Hawaii when there are no hurricanes? I have to go check it out.

(Tomorrow—which is actually next year in your time, dear reader.)
Coffee scratched me in the eye again. That is the anklet's name. *Side note: *she* corrected me. She wants everyone to understand that she is not a bracelet. She says proudly, "An-ke-let, yes!"

Well, neither of them will let me catch them, the Ankle nor Coffee the Anklet. She only dances with me and does well to keep her distance on each step. She says the lady never really cared about her. Never took her to Sephora for their special body scrub sales. Never even tried testing a lil' of the old *Beautiful* perfume on her.

Coffee says people on Earth in your time take ankles for granted. Coffee says ankles like perfume along with kisses in the dark and sometimes, if the mood is right, butter. Got to be Land-O-Lakes though. That is the stuff ankles live for, Land-O-Lakes butter and feathery touches under dinner tables between les aperitifs and whatever else the party orders to dine on. Ankles get tired of hauling around all the weight you know, without even hearing a thank you or being covered well in the wintertime. They say they hate being stuck in stiletto all the time, too. And they hate guys with high-topped boots because they get rashes from always being rubbed the wrong way.

So the ankle, Coffee and I are all dancing and a kind man with soft perplexing whiskers saddles next to us. He is upside down and I am worried. I have gas and he is a bit too near my behind region and I think he just grazed my butt cheek with a whisker. "I cannot smell," he reassures me and we continue dancing and include him on the next song that lasts four earth days. No wonder everyone up here is in shape. I can get used to living here. There are glittery wigs that turn into any of your wishes and paintings on every star and Black people do not get called monkey's and uncivilized and women dance naked and free without anyone rolling camcorders for internet sales and the men do not just sit on the sidelines and watch, they join in and everyone says thank you and greets you with real smiles even if they are toothless and 200 years old and the old do not squeak like tin, instead they move like grape jam and they do not hate their offspring because the young people on the Moon chose to wear human styled clothing and listen to music unlike that of their long gone teenaged years.

Things move everyway but down here.

The only thing the Moon people are unhappy about is that whole man on the Moon business.

Let me explain. Sonya filled me in and she doesn't usually talk but I told her you'd want to hear this.

That first man on the Moon thing was all a hoax. He never came here. His voyage to outer space was no great act of heroism and it for damn sure wasn't on the tip of magnanimous exploration. Nope. The real deal was that he and his wife, Muni (pronounced: Money), had gotten into a real fiasco because he'd lied to her about giving up cigars. He was going to the garage and smoking those miniature cancer-causing logs every evening. The argument turned so ugly Muni left and came back up here to her people. To truly understand this whole thing, you need to know: they'd never argued before. Not even one time. Not even over the toilet seat being left up or the way he threw his undies next to the wicker laundry basket. Muni didn't know what to do about this huge flare up. It was pretty bad. Shoes got chewed up, a brick got thrown at the garage door—clearly tens years of bottled up name calling and fault finding let on the loose.

What if they ended up like Raymond's parents on that one show, so mean and terrible to each other, never sharing a kind word? Moon people are very not like humans. The Moon ones do not know how to handle such bittered love even though they look a lot like us earthlings--except their blood is crystal clear.

Whenever one of them comes down to Earth they dye their blood by drinking four gallons of pure cranberry juice—the bitter, non-diluted kind from the health food store--so they won't be killed or experimented on or hated for mere difference, as is human custom. "Some humans will hate you simply because you exist. Earth is beautiful but that is the reason I do not miss it," Muni still says.

Then too, Muni missed seeing everyone back home. Like her best friend Adelaide. Adelaide came down without tainting her blood and *man* was that a mistake. The NRPTGU (Nuclear ? People That Go Unknown) kept her in the lab for three years until she finally figured out how to escape. It was sort of like that movie *Splash* but worse for reasons I cannot disclose. Anywho, Adelaide is paying the bastards back by sending down Moon Maidens. Moon Maidens always cause human men to go blind.

Muni was having fun reconnecting with Adelaide and her parents and kicking her feet up in the cheesecake dust—that is what their ground taste like. And you can eat the dirt, it's cheesecake too. Some patches with cherries. Some without. Sometimes with lemon or frothy icing that whitens teeth.

But she couldn't take watching her hubby down below. He tossed and turned all night and kept his dress shoes on even when he went to bed or got in the shower and he didn't even noticed he was doing it; he was terribly preoccupied with her departure. What if she was divorcing him? How would they split the kids? That thought ran thru his head every hour at work.

Muni decided it would be in both their best interest to communicate with each other so she sent him a message that was extra lovey-dovey and he heard her words that night and the next morning he went outside in backyard of their home in D.C. and looked at to the blue sky. His shoes shook off his feet and he closed his eyes, opened them and became completely invisible to earthling man as Muni's energy sucked him in. It felt good. He shot up and propelled higher and higher into the air, faster than any aircraft force back then had ever dared to travel. And he didn't have to worry about explosion. Even if he would have had to worry about explosion, he would have had to try it if he wanted Muni back. She wasn't about to come down. She hated the way the government tapped into people's phone conversations with outer space, add the fact that she'd asked him more than too many times to quit that smoking indulgence of his. And their kids. Those bad ass kids! They were always eating her cell phone when she left it on the coffee table—she was on her seventh one now, they were always stealing the teachers chalk in school and bringing it home to play four squares on the sidewalk and making up songs that made Muni wonder if they were full of the devil—if mixing the bloods was really a bad thing. Her husband wasn't going to mind leaving *them* behind--that was for sure. Besides, Muni was scaring them straight at night while they were asleep. The oldest, Kim hadn't bitten her teachers for a whole month. Yes, Muni could keep a good eye on her little rascals from the Moon.

"Honey, slow it down a bit," he shouted to Muni and Muni slowed the speed of his departure. I can totally understand that. Things like breezing into space, you don't want to rush thru life altering events such as those. When you actually reach the sky, you pop thru to outer space—it's exactly like when you're chewing bubble gum and you blow a bubble but the bubble burst open a little leaving a hole in the tip. The only difference is Earth doesn't sag and crumble away like gum.

That brings me to another thought. It's a little off the subject but, not really. Earth only gets all that attention because she is fragile. It's only a matter of time, if the red blooded ones don't stop acting crazy, before earth gets tired and gives out. She's already done that twice now and word has it she told Mars and the whole population of Red people along with some Saturnites of planet Saturn the Stern Wheeled Sat (that's the planets real name) that that's what it's coming down to. All that fighting going on deep inside her stomach is giving her hypertension and ulcers. Normally earth has a strong constitution–what, with all that water and air floating around.

Anyway, Earth is so used to all the attention she gets now. Sat says part of her threats of giving out and dying are from her addiction to attention. Think about it. People don't go around giving out Your Well cards—only Get Well Soon ones. And family members that've been estranged over inheritance arguments and antique tea kettles that weren't willed to them, those type of relatives don't stop by just to say hi 'cause they heard you were well. They only come over if they hear thru the one relative they *are* still speaking to that Aunt So-in-So is ill—even if the visit *is* secretly only with the hope that Aunt So-in-So will put them in her will. They come from out of town even. But not if you are well and have food in the fridge and your marriage is in tact! That's just the way it goes. Earth's got a good point in getting all she can out of a bad health condition.

Now is a good time for me to tell you. Moon wishes to inform all humans of her real name: Moon'Na. We've gotten it wrong for so long. She is very sassy and actually cursed me out for calling her The Moon but I will spare you the details. She's very fond of the Ankle and Coffee but I think she has something against humans like me. But how was I supposed to know her real name?

I know, I know, I've done you like the evening news. I've teased you with the story but here it goes and you should get it more now that I have given you some background info.

The only reason they made that big ole whooptie do about the man landing on Moon/Moon'Na is because of this: It looked like Muni's husband, Mikey Clark, was mysteriously killed. With info like that spreading everyone was saying he was involved in bad business, if you know what I mean. He had been so involved in the elections and practically lived in Congress, it just didn't look good. And it was leaking out that Muni (who had changed her name to Mary for the sake of her earthly life) was in fact from the Moon—one of those people the government was still debating as to whether they were terrorists or freaks. This is hard on Moon'Na people, living on Earth. Not just because of the labeling. I have learned from my time up here that, after three years or so, although they maintain their intelligence, they forget everything--except their names, their family and other 'Na people. It's hard to remain undercover when you've forgotten why you have to be undercover.

When Mikey Clark came up here, he loved it so much. ...The Snookie Snevitas and Larkie Lads who loved making sugared rain dough and wearing colorful plaids, all different types of homemade dinners, toppling kempa trees, the parks without dog droppings, the way he could jump from one planet to another—he didn't even mind Muni dancing naked with the other 'Na people. At night she was always with him in their cozy house made out of circular ice cubes and playing cards. He was sincerely upset with Muni for hiding her heritage from him.

Everyone thought he was just putting on at first. I came here for a different reason—for the ankle. When Mikey Clark came everyone thought it was to try to make Muni go back down to Earth and to pretend she was human again. 'Na's think there is not enough misery up here for humans to function properly on Moon'Na the way Mikey was doing. They say humans are not happy without some great form of tragedy; the sadness preoccupies earthlings from boredom.

And since life on Moon'Na was so great, Mikey Clark did not come back. The children, Kim, Savittie, and Dang, they eventually came up too.

So, to throw all the attention off Mikey Clark's disappearance, they sent Neil Armstrong in great earthly fashion. Now that I have been up here I know the shuttle thing was a total waste of money. (If you close your eyes and imagine—without trying too hard, though—you can touch my hand right now. Try it. Wait. You're doing it incorrectly. There…that's it, there you go…see. You smell nice and I like the way you're wearing you hair).

Moon'Na people try not to laugh at their earthly sisters and brothers but sometimes they cannot help it. They are still cracking up about that picture of Neil Armstrong with that flag posted on top of Moon'Na's head. Earthly governments didn't even ask Moon'Na or them if they would mind. They just hitched the cloth up here--supposedly.

Mr. Armstrong didn't come here either. He just closed his eyes and imagined just like you can do and the NRPTGU took what he said he'd imagined and ran with it.

Moon'Na is strong and unlike Earth though they are sisters. She would not let Neil or anyone else come and snap pictures of her without her consent and she definitely wouldn't let anyone thwack all over her with flag poles and stuff.

34.

on the illegal mexican subject:

Dear Illegal Mexicans. I have gotten into so much trouble over you. All because I spoke out and said some things Black females are not supposed to say. I have made some people very, very mad and while I do not care, I do think this issue needs to be resolved so that we do not have to go down this road again.

Here we sit at the negotiation table, a representative for Illegal Mexicans, the mediator and myself.

Me—
I would first like to say, thank you for coming.

Illegal Rep, Ms. White—
(blank stare)

Me—
Ok my problem is, you are people of color and yet and still some of you talk about Black people just as bad as some of the color-less do. I don't think it's right. I heard this one guy say on the train one time, 'Don't think Black, don't think White, think Mexicano!' While I would be the first to say you should be proud of your own, why you gotta hate on us? We've been here all along, we were brought here yet some of you try to act like Black folks are nothing. And whenever I say something about this situation, everybody trips. It's not cool.

Illegal Rep, Ms. White—
You are a racist.

Me—
Not even a bigot, please believe. You are not trying to understand what I am saying.

Illegal Rep, Ms. White—

You are a racist.

Me—
Good example: there was a song this one guy wrote in Spanish about a popular Black guy doggin' him and talkin' about the sweatshops he uses for his clothing line. Why not include all the companies that use kids for cheap labor including him?

Illegal Rep, Ms. White—
You are prejudiced and small minded.

Me—
Okay. Let's try it from a different angle. What about my friend in high school that was Puerto Rican? Her dad told me one day when I was at their house that he could not stand Blacks… His hair was curlier than mine. What's up with that?

Illegal Rep, Ms. White—
You are mean and racist.

Me—
Okay, okay. What about this? Why not recognize all that Black folks done that enough for all people of color in the world?

Illegal Rep, Ms. White—
(blank stare)

Me—
Don't you see? When you are here working under the table, you're getting gypped. Some people think Mexicans are supposed to serve them. Its exploitation. You wanna know how I know? I had a boyfriend that wasn't of color once tell me that you all help the economy. That's the same shit they said about slavery. Why not ban together with us Black folk?

Illegal Rep, Ms. White—
Mexicans are not Black…

Me—
Why not help try to help the people in Sudan get US residency too? They're being killed as we speak.

Illegal Rep, Ms. White—
You are a racist.

Me—
I guess the plan is working. Not just on the Blackies. Some of you are falling for it all, too…

Illegal Rep, Ms. White—
Why must it always be race this and race that with you?

Me—
I give up. We're gonna be back in slavery times real soon. Probably in the next two years. And don't ask me to help you find no Harried Tubman either. Go 'head and ban together with the ones that want you to keep making 20 cents on tha dollar. Us Black folk done moved up to sit down security jobs now. We done quit mopping up Neimans… In a minute your brothas are gonna be rappin' sayin' Latino bitches ain't shit and the brown folks are gonna be complaining about your men all being put in jail or caught up in the system…

The Mediator--
(turns to Illegal Rep) Let's go. She's crazy…

*This meeting was held six months before Affirmative Action was revoked.

35.

the most wonderfulest thing

The most wonderful thing occurs
when one runs into one who understands
without words or suitable gestures,
when glances replace dictionaries

however,
should such an incident not occur
the most wonderfulest thing is achieved
when one understands her or himself…

36.

wylie's faith

I'm sick and tired of all these weird ass stories ahead of mine by these weird ass, not quite right people who think they're real. If they aren't out of touch with reality I don't know *who* is!

Later for all of them and their jacked up heads. I've got this one problem. I keep doing stupid stuff and I am *so* tired of jacking myself up. I just went on a blind date and man was it terrible. My friend thought we'd hit it off. WRONG! I did everything a person could possibly do to turn a guy off. Not on purpose though. I had bad breath—but wait a minute! Let me explain. I had just brushed my teeth and you know how if you don't eat anything after you brush your teeth, your breath starts smelling all weird like too much peroxide or something? Yeah, I had *that* going on. Then my hair had gotten all messed up in the rain and I had done my makeup in bad lighting and my girl said it looked like I had mistaken blush for face powder.

And he was a guy that really wasn't that fly so that only made things worse. I made myself look terrible in front of someone that wasn't even on my level. He still thinks black leather sectional couches and vertical blinds are en vogue for heavens sake! Could somebody please tell Black folk all over America that the look is played! Its 'bout as played as that *Golden Girls* peach and sea green get-up old people like to decorate their houses with like they're in Florida and it's still 1989.

I could have done *way* better than this blind date dude.

Anyhow, now I have decided to take control of my life from now on. I am tired of barely living pay check ta pay check on this neo-plantation some call a department store and not being who I was created on this earth to be! Tonight I'm gonna wish for everything I ever wanted... It's a full moon tonight and, oh, I'm *gonna* get what I want! Watch.

Two years later with no recollection of the wish/spell/prayer (whatever makes you comfortable)...

"Where's our waiter? I need another drink."
"Okay!" Krista toasted my Cosmo with her Baileys on the rocks. "The boutique is bangin' girl! Next week I've scheduled an appointment for you with Man-Man Designs. He's been itchin' ta get his line in Posh Revenue."
"You think the line is high end enough for us?"
"*Man-Man*? Do-I-think-*Man-Man*-is-high-end-enough? Wylie, sometimes I swear you live under a rock somewhere in the Netherlands. He's on this year's Fortune 500 list and he's been featured in *Vibe* three times within the last two years. And *he* is dying to get *his* stuff in *your* store!"
"Well...I'll take a look at what he's got."
"I wanna keep us original. I didn't make my thirteen million by carrying the same stuff all the other stores down the block have on their shelves."
"Well...I'll let you handle things your way but, don't be too snobby when you meet with him. I mean, just because you live on South Beach and own a condo building and one of the world's most famous boutique doesn't mean you have to come off like you're better than everyone else." Krista snickered and shook her head.
"Yeah, life's been good to me."
"I'd say. How did you do it? How did you make it all happen, I mean?"
"What? You're a *True Hollywood Story* reporter now or something?"
"Well...you might actually be on there one day..." Krista always knows how to flatter. Then again, when you're considered a major anomaly and success, who doesn't?
"Hmm...I don't know. I work hard to get what I want. I guess I'm just blessed.

37.

3 facts to be proud of

Yes. Even though I am a makeup queen and at times can alter my voice into an octave deeper than that of some men, I was born female and will continue to remain as such.

Yes. The real name's Mianne Adufutse.

No. Everything a writer writes is not always about his or her own life. Many times the words and stories come from places deep within imaginings, therefore I find the imagination to be the most dangerous and exciting thing around.

38.

da ghetto children

My girl, Co-Tan (if you suspected a fake name, you'd be correct) is very smart.

The other day we were on the phone and she said something that made me think.
"Tha ghetto children are going to be the ones to live the longest," she stated.
"Why do you say that?" I asked.
"Because. They aren't sittin' in air conditioning all day, playing video games and getting obese. All these young kids have diabetes and stuff nowadays. But the ghetto kids are outside playing and having fun because that's all they can afford to do. They're gonna be the healthiest."

39.

the reason i say some of the things i do

if pink
don't like no shade uh black
and brown
don't wanna git down wit black
cause pink say black
is whack
and red
got busted in da head
fa bein' in open spaces—
american places
and yellow
got sad faces
cause pink
say yellow cain't think
--uh lil' bit uh black
still make 'em tainted

how come we all
wudden't made blue?
if pink was blue
pink would feel
just like all the other colors do…

Blackie stay back

…But really it's not really like that
we like Black
you aren't wack

special thanks
to your mental slacking,
for are pockets are never left lacking…

40. or… #1? Hmm…

dear goddess,

I am writing this letter to you because I feel so bad for you. No one remembers you and it has to feel worse than God forgetting your birthday and your anniversary! Or your name! And whenever someone mentions you, they automatically get blacklisted like they're a hexing witch or something. Everyone remembers your son. But not you dear, beautiful Goddess. Your name doesn't even have to be capitalized. Spell check won't even highlight you uncapitalized. That's really got to suck—whoops, my bad, dear, oh dear, sweet, beautiful Goddess, my other creator.

Hmm.

People are more familiar with Britney Spears than they are with you. I would say that was one up for Brittney but, since you are Goddess, I cannot take that liberty.

Lovely Goddess, I would like to get to know you better. I always include you in prayer. But I don't know if it's okay to switch and say "Goddess and God and their son and daughter—if you have either." Other times I say, "God and Goddess and their son and daughter or daughters and maybe sons?"

I think I will say "Goddess and God and their children" from now on. That way, I cover all your kids and the ones on earth I normally wouldn't pray for.

One time this guy thought I was trying to say God is a transvestite. No. I don't even think you two are the same person. I have never seen a man have a baby. Or a woman have one by herself. I am unsure about Mary. The conclusions aren't in on that one for me just yet. Miracles do happen. I'm typing this right now. I used to hate typing. Now it's one of my less guiltier pleasures. Typing. The stroking of the keys. The tapping sound. The output…yeah, typing is one of the good things in life. And it's a miracle that I finally started liking it. See the power good teachers and instructors have?

But back to you dear neglected Mother. I have been thinking about writing this letter for a long time. Not only so I could type something up. No. Because one time I had this really hot idea and I kept thinking it couldn't be God. A man wouldn'ta come up with that idea. Not even if he was gay—and I have had a lot of good, gay male guy friends—I should know. And I had been thinking about that whole trinity and holy spirit and Mary thing anyway. Since I was eight years old sitting in a place something like a church.

How are you, good Goddess? How do you feel? Do you mind if I start talking to you more often? I wouldn't think you would mind, not getting called on as much as I am sure you do not but you may be accustomed to this lack of bother and disturbance by now. Hey, you may not want to be called upon! And that would really suck for me. Whoops—my bad. See, I need you in my life, dear Goddess. Look at all this slippery language going on. I am a bad girl but I would like to be good sometimes. Are you a bad woman, too, wonderful, oh wonderful, loving Goddess? Or are you always good and that is why no one remembers you? Even men can't stand good girls. They claim they like them but they still dip out with the bad ones every now and again. And God is not always good. He pays people back and stuff. But I guess he has to. He is God. But even then, I guess he is too nice sometimes too because he lets the sun shine on the evil just as well. But then again, good people die all the time. But then again maybe that is not so bad if they are heaven or Florida bound.

I am thinking a lot of people in Florida are already dead because they look like movie stars even when they are just regular people who live in Florida *and* because some of them are so old. It's like a Mecca for old people. I am also thinking Florida is *heaven*. Hmm…I should move there very soon then, in that case. If you and God will let me. I have not always been working towards that heavenly light, if you know what I mean. But…I am cleaning up my act. See. I contacted you, right?

Well. Although they don't say much about you at most churches, dear oh, dear oh, sweet Goddess, I would love to change that sad but true fact. After all, you are everywhere. Why shouldn't you be talked about in your own house?

Well. That is it for now. But tonight I have a list of concerns I would love to go over with you. Wait. Wait a minute. My bad. I am being selfish. I will wait for you to tell me and show me more about all that is Goddess first.

Sincerely,
One Who Does Not Wish To Remain Lost

41.

ménage a whoops

The wise buster
overtly taking it upon himself
to declare pimp status for talking
his girl into the much merited threesome
would do well to consider exactly what he shall do
if and when she should
from that point on
remain untrue
in favor of
la cou

42.

american steal machine

Casts:
US Machine aka "Controller"
Shaharia (Sha-har-ree-uh)-an attractive twenty four year old, African American woman that looks weary and worn down past her years

At Rise:
A rainy day in Washington D.C. at the top of the Pentagon

Controller
Ma lady, make your statement quick! Since you are twenty-four, I will allow you twenty-four nano seconds.

Shaharia
Wh-hat? I have traveled from New York, to Russia, then Detroit, then some hick town next to Waco, Texas, over to New Orleans after the hurricane incident and, now that they have finally allowed me to come here, you are only giving me nanoseconds? I will not accept this!

Controller
You have ten left nano's left, ma lady!

Shaharia
Wait! It took me two years just to get into the House of Legislation and another year just to stand before you today, here in the Pentagon! I have had to wait here for months in a line. I've been treated like an experiment. They made us play creative games just to see how smart we were. The smartest ones were annihilated after a month or so while the ones they found less intellectual escaped death. What is this? All I wanted to do was talk to Bush and Clinton—

Controller
The Presidents, my lady, Presidents. No more nanoseconds. Goodbye.

Shaharia
NO! NO! *(moves closer)* Wait! You are a machine? A machine? I cannot believe I waited for three years, leaving my family behind without so much as a note telling them of my journey only to find out that the person or people in charge of the United States of America are--or shall I say—IS a machine!

Controller
This is obviously why you weren't killed off during the first round… Yes! Yes, ma lady! I am a machine. Seems like my voice would have given me away a long while ago, aye?

Shaharia
But—but, this is a land of people! Live human beings! If you won't allow me to make my plea (steps closer), I will tell everyone that our country is controlled by a shiny machine! I will tell them how you torture all those that come to you for answers concerning our government! I will tell them how you kill those that are "too smart"! And I will tell them how to reach you. I'll tell them that you sit on top of the Pentagon! I'll tell them, I swear I will!

Controller
Oh, you stupid little human person! *(Laughs)* We kill you stupid humans everyday-- cigarettes, MTV, BET, cocaine, religion and with our games of war, the list goes on and on. Really. There is no reason for war, I am friends with Iraq's machines, Sierra Leone's machines, Russia's machines, Japan, the G8—we are all *"cool,"* as is the terminology you Black ones and White one's like to use. You humans are so stupid, you never pay attention to anything past the given. Humans commit suicide with their own stupidity. You all really are cute *(attempts to use his handle to rub her nose)*.

Shaharia
(moves out of reach).

Controller
For some reason, you intrigue my numerical data. I have yet to meet a human like yourself. Usually they all shake and tremble in my presence and forget what it is what they came here to say. Okay. What have you to say?

Shaharia
Look. For decades and centuries people have suffered. But, at this point, it is unbearable. Women are still not given the same pay as men, women are still treated as second-class citizens, men still treat women as objects—and truthfully, if it was fair, I wouldn't mind. If there were commercials for porno's entitled, *Boys at College Gone Wild,* I wouldn't even be upset, but there aren't-- women are continually objectified. And when that occurs, it becomes sexism. And finally: racism. It has to stop. Black people are truly suffering. Just like Simple stated in one of Langston Hughes short stories, foreigners can come to America and get more freedom than a Black person. Foreigners never had to sit in the back of a bus. And they were never lynched on American soil!

Controller
Oh, yes, yes…Langston…he was getting in the way…that's why he died a bit early, hmm…

Shaharia
What did you say?

Controller
Never mind. You like Langston, hmm? What about the Yin Yang twins? Now they are hot, if I must say so myself. I put them out there along with Snoop, 2 Live Crew and Jay Z.

Shaharia
You put them out there?

Controller
Yes. See, it is all about the numbers. I'm a machine, right? All I care about are the numbers. Young boys listen to Snoop and desire

to be pimps, young girls listen to Yin Yang Twins and want to become 'hoes' instead of vital, functioning parts of the family unit and society. Take slavery for instance. It really was not anything for you or your people to take personally. Someone needed this land. The people already on it wouldn't move so, Christopher tried to be nice to them and asked those Indian people to work for him but, as you humans have the terrible curse of emotion, they would not cooperate. Besides, when they did work for him, they barely did anything outside of admiring the sun and clouds and sung songs in voices worse than mine. They weren't productive. So they had to be annihilated. One African could do the same amount of work as three of them. Now that's something for you Black people to be proud of. Isn't that what humans want, something to be proud of?

Shaharia
I want equal rights for women and Black people. I figure, since the US is on top right now, all other countries will follow suit, then there would be worldwide equality.

Controller
That is what you have traveled these three years for, ma lady?

Shaharia
Yes!

Controller
Well…it is not that easy although, these wishes of yours may very well be doable…but it will cost you…

Shaharia
I'm ready to make a deal.

Controller
Okay. Six for six billion. I want that guy friend of yours with the Malcolm X glasses.

Shaharia
My boyfriend? Yusef?

Controller
Yes, him—do not interrupt me! That friend of yours that always goes around speaking at churches and talks a bit like Martin Luther King... The girl you always pass out those feminist flyers with that has with the fro—sort of like Angela Davis--that one. The skinny boy, what is his name? Oh yes, yes David Chappelle. And that new kid, kanye West. Bring all of them to me. This time I will not make you wait in line. In fact, you can take the jet and you all should be here in no less than two hours.

Shaharia
And what happens after that?

Controller
Well, I will kill all of you. I will put you in the furnace and you use as fuel.

Shaharia
What? You say it so matterfactly! Kill us? Don't you think that's a bit harsh?

Controller
Well, ma lady, we will make it look like two separate assassinations for David Chappelle and Kanye, you know. For you and the others, we will simply write a nationwide article about all of you and how dedicated to human rights you all were.

Shaharia
How do you figure?

Controller
You all get your claim to fame and together, your six lives are worth six billion since the other in the masses are not as—how shall I put it—not as aware. It's all in the numbers. It all has to balance out.

Shaharia

Well if we are more aware…once you kill us, would equal rights really matter? No. I am willing to give up my life but not in vain. If I die in such a manner, I want to know that my death meant something, that the masses would gain something—not lose something vital.

Controller

You really do think you are important, don't you?

Shaharia

I'm not dumb. I know how to act the part but, trust me, I ain't no dummy. You want to use me for fuel. You want to study my mind. *You* think I'm important, that's why you want me dead!

Controller

Oh, you Blacks and your slang! 'Ain't' is one of my favorite word choices you all use! Say it again, just one more time!

Shaharia

I'm not about to let you turn me into a coon bafoon. I speak like myself but, at the same time, I'm not here to humor you with Ebonics. My people came here and weren't allowed to read, or be educated. Considering all that we did well to learn English to the best of our ability.

Controller

Just one time, Please!

Shaharia

Funny, everybody needs Black folks to entertain them yet y'all hate us so.

Controller

You said *Y'all*! Say it again! I love it! I love it!

Shaharia

Look. I'm not gonna—

Controller
--*Gonna!* You said Gonna! And you said it so *Black*! I love it! Say it again!

Shaharia
You are missing the point. You're trying to use diversion to butter me up and evade coming to a mutual agreement...

Controller
No, no. I think you Blacks are the best dancers, singers, sport players we've got in the world today.

Shaharia
Okay. Now I see why the country is ran in such a racist, inefficient manner! You're ignorant. Not only are we good entertainers, we, you hear me, WE came up with Egyptian Mysticism the Greeks copied. We were the first philosophers, the first civilized, the first to discover math and pie and brain surgery. And after all that, your other machines decided to teach us that we came from monkey's and were uncivilized beasts until Christopher and his friends decided to enslave us! I will not lie down here and die to supply you with fuel. You know what? You need me! You need *us*! And that is why you treat women and Black people like dirt. It's basic psychology. Give us low self-worth, get what you want for low costs. But it *is* costing you something. This mistreatment is costing the world something.

Controller
Oh, she is not dumb after all, hmm. But one thing you miss, ma lady, a good story needs conflict. If I give you what you want, me and the other machines will have nothing else to watch and amused ourselves with!

Shaharia
Look. Let's make an agreement. We give women and Black people equal rights and dignity and banish racism and sexism. Fair and square. You get recognition amongst all the other machines.

Controller
No! Show me that lil Black punanny of yours, then… then, I'd be willing to do it! Equality for your Blacks and women! I'd do it!

Shaharia
I am not even offended by your ignorance anymore. I will have to find a way to do this on my own. Forget it. I won't die for you (walks out).

Controller
She did not try to kill me, she did not even cry…hmmm… We'd better watch her. She may very well be too powerful, even for me. (To stage left) Bush! Bush? I need a tracking device on that one that just exited, pronto!

43.

nothing

Don't go nowhere outside dey own neighborhood, don't try nothing new, don't like nothing dat ain't like them, don't know nothing 'cause…dey nothing—dem nothings. Don't like people dat spend up all dey time tryin' ta be something, dey don't care 'bout nothing. Dem nothings? Dey just sit around and do nothing all day; oh, yeah, and dey want you ta do nothing right along wit 'em. Dey don't smile at nothing but nothing, don't want nothing, don't believe in nothing…'cause dey nothingness. and the nothings don't want dey kids ta want nothing, dey don't talk about nothing. Dem nothings, dey think something is really nothing.

something

Somethings got to believe in something, something makes them better. The somethings have something and something always takes them places, where something goes is very far and that is why the nothings call them stars. Somethings breathe in purity, love being a something's only way. For somethings know they are something more than mere, breathing dust. The somethings are that they are, all that is. Somethings laugh and find delight in everything, for them something is not all.

44.

bootleg woman

spunky
and funky

but
(guess what?)
something wrong when a chick don't fly…

45.

a sticky note for it because there is nothing else to say

> you used to be hugging
> me
>
> now you just straight
> the fuck up bugging me

46.

spankikie (spank-kah-kee)

a favorite word in the language of the people on my planet

47.

the toki violet

The minute she was old enough she changed her name to The Toki Violet--and yes, the 'The' was included. Violet Green was way too 7-Up cake, collard green, prune eating, wedding reception in the basement of the mall, 70 year old, everyday church going, catching the bus or waiting for a jitney kind of old lady name.

She was gonna be a rock star. She said that one day we each took turns pushing her swing in the park on the corner of our block. She listened to Barbie and the Rockers everyday after school.

We didn't argue her point. She was Toki (she made us start calling her that in the fourth grade). But everybody and they mama said, outside of her Black Barbie lookin' looks, she wasn't going nowhere.

LaLisa's granny said, "She outta be tryin' ta be herself sum kinda nurse. Na dat's uh nice job fa uh girl like dat. Sho is prettie." Everyone always said that about Toki. She was five nine and a half, light skinned and had long, reddish brown hair that—although it was nappy—people saw potential in hair of that length. "Where she git dat frum?" all the grannies on the block wondered. "Musta been dat ole no good bastard dat had da nerve ta do dat ta Fareen. Dat Fareen Green hadn't been much uh no kinda looker--dem big goggly glasses and da kinda hair that wasn't even 'nuff ta make uh tuff on da back uh her neck." And black. Lord that po' woman were black. "Black as tar, cursin' ya eyes lessen you at da bar," Mr. Mitchell, the neighborhood's version of Norm quipped about Toki's mother who'd left the baby with Grandma Green before her second birthday. No one even knew where Fareen was. No one, not even Toki, cared. Some things were better left alone. Like Toki. Who hated that her granny used the Bridge card like it was going out of style. "If da govnment gon' gimme somen fa free, I'm sho gon' take it! I done worked on dey cotton fields an' paid dem outta ma check evry week!" Grandma Green ain't care.

But Toki did. What kind of a lifestyle was that for a future star? And she knew, she just knew she was going to be one day. She had even gotten granny used to calling her Toki and Grandma Green was one of those old schooled old ladies that didn't believe in no chile tellin' her nothing. Children were supposed to be seen and not heard. But Toki always got to her, just like granny's good ole snuff.

I guess all her hard work, all those weekends spent in Toki's basement listening to her rendition of "Every Rose Has Its Stone" and acting like Molly Ringwald and walking to the bus stop listening to guys tell her "Cute ass ta stop," then yelling as they passed by that she was "Too weird wit all dat pink hair." (Then Pink the singer came out and she got picked to be the captain of the cheerleading squad because she was so, "Aheada her time."). All that time spent rewinding recordings of Grammy and BET award shows. All those hours spent listening to Mary J. Blige and Diana Ross and Michael and his sister and all those hours spent huddled under the cover with the flashlight and the *Vogue* fashion and *Vibe* magazines Granny Green said were, "Worldly and gon' head her straight ta hell on skis," all the days spent working at Hardee's and memorizing words to lyrics while operating the drive thru after cheerleading practice til 12 in the morning and not getting her nails done because she had to save, all the hours practicing with the choir and listening to the saved ones who hated that "Damn pank haya dat ain't have no business sangin' fa da Lord," all those days spent keeping her wish to herself outside of her weekend audience which consisted of me, M'Cretia and LaLisa, all of that must have finally paid off because when I was flipping thru channels looking for that one ice skating special after I went to the kitchen to get some cookies during the commercial break, I heard Toki's voice and stopped dead in my tracks. "December. Are you ready?"

I ran back into the living room and caught her face right before the next commercial flashed on. Her album? Her album! Next was her face on every billboard off all the high ways leading to the city. I just couldn't believe it.

Here I was sitting on my couch while she was somewhere in New York or LA or wherever it is singers live, living it up. I wanted to be jealous of her. I wanted to hope her all the worst things. Like a one hit wonder song and being dissed by Wendy Williams in a magazine.

But I couldn't. The Toki Violet was still my girl.

A week later my cousin Nate came from the mailbox with a cream envelope stuck between the sales papers and he shoved it in my hand:

Dear Tessa,

How have you been? I am pretty sure you are fine. Sorry I left without saying anything. I didn't want granny to find out—you know she never would have let me go. I'm living in New York now. Granny tripped at first but now she's fine. She still won't come visit though, but at least she's speaking to me now. I sent her some pictures so she'd finally believe that I'm well and alive.

Things are great. I'd really like you to visit. Will you come? Call me and let me know. If you can, and I truly hope you can, I'll send your ticket info to your email.

Sincerely,
The Toki Violet
212.222.0765

And that was the beginning of The Toki Violet Files...

www.ingramcontent.com/pod-product-compliance
Ingram Content Group UK Ltd.
Pitfield, Milton Keynes, MK11 3LW, UK
UKHW041950230426
12048UKWH00008B/256